Amelia seemed to snap out of it. She looked directly at him. She seemed nervous. Her voice took on a new, quiet quality.

"Helen was right, you know. I *was* jealous of you going out with her."

Kevin froze. It seemed like, in that moment, their whole world had changed. Amelia was standing over two feet away from him, but he was sure that he could hear the loud thud of her heartbeat, that she could hear his.

"She was right about me, too," he whispered. "Most of it, anyway."

Kevin stared into Amelia's eyes. He could feel his chin trembling. It was a feeling he'd never had before. He wondered if it showed.

"So what are we going to do about it?" Amelia asked, softly, uncertainly.

Later, neither of them could be sure who made the first move. All they knew was how they were in each other's arms, kissing so hard that it almost hurt.

Point Romance

Cradle Snatcher

Alison Creaghan

Cover illustration by
Derek Brazell

■SCHOLASTIC

Scholastic Children's Books,
Scholastic Publications Ltd,
7-9 Pratt Street, London NW1 OAE, UK

Scholastic Inc.,
555 Broadway, New York, NY 10012-3999, USA

Scholastic Canada Ltd,
123 Newkirk Road, Richmond Hill,
Ontario, Canada L4C 3G5

Ashton Scholastic Pty Ltd,
P O Box 579, Gosford, New South Wales,
Australia

Ashton Scholastic Ltd,
Private Bag 92801, Penrose, Auckland,
New Zealand

First published by Scholastic Children's Books, 1993

Text copyright © Alison Creaghan, 1993
Cover illustration copyright © Derek Brazell, 1993

ISBN 0 590 55278 3

Typeset by Wyvern Typesetting Ltd, Bristol
Printed by Cox & Wyman Ltd, Reading, Berks

Contents

August

1

It wasn't a bad wedding, as weddings go. The cere-
mony took less than an hour, but then the endless
photographs began. The sun peered uncertainly
through the clouds as Kirsty and Brian posed this
way, that way, any way the photographer asked.
Amelia, standing around with the rest of the
guests, found the whole business irritating and
unnatural. But the bride and groom looked
happy. So, she guessed, none of the rest mattered.

"Ah, ain't they sweet," a familiar voice teased
from behind her.

"Very romantic," Amelia replied.

She spoke in a sarcastic tone even though she
meant it sincerely. Kevin Atkinson often had that
effect on her. He was a blonde-haired, blue-eyed
boy a year younger than her. Amelia was nearly
sixteen.

"Can't see why they bothered getting married,
really," Kevin said, smiling. "After all, they've
been living together for two years."

"You'll understand when you're older," Amelia
teased him back.

She went to pat Kevin on the head, the way she'd been doing since he was two. But then she stopped. Even though Amelia was wearing one-and-a-half inch heels, Kevin was the same height as her. Oh well, she thought. That had to happen sooner or later. She was five-four, and had been for eighteen months.

"I hope they get a move on," Kevin told her. "I'm starving."

As he spoke, the photographer called for friends of the bride. Kevin, blue eyes sparkling, went where he was told. Amelia stayed where she was.

Coddington wasn't a very big village. Nearly everyone knew everyone else. But Amelia's family were closer to Brian's parents than to Kirsty's, so she had to wait to appear in that photo. While she was watching, Steve Hooper, who used to go to her school, sauntered over.

"You're looking great today, Amelia."

"Thank you."

Amelia didn't return the compliment. She didn't fancy Steve – a tall, rather greasy, medical student – but he clearly fancied himself.

"I'm looking forward to getting you on the dance floor tonight."

Amelia gave Steve what she hoped was a wry smile. Why was it that some boys thought the fact that they went to university meant you should be flattered when they tried to chat you up?

"You'll have to get past my boyfriend first," she told him.

Before Steve could respond, the photographer called for friends of the groom. Steve grabbed her arm. Amelia was forced to pose next to him, a forced grin on her face. I hope Mum and Dad don't buy a copy of this photo, she thought.

At last it was all over. Amelia avoided the bouquet, which was caught by the bride's sister, Helen. Helen was a pretty girl with long, blonde hair and slim athletic legs. She was a year younger than Amelia.

"Please don't throw confetti on the grass," the vicar pleaded. "Despite what it says on the packets, the birds *don't* eat it."

But he was ignored. Cameras flashed as multi-coloured shards of paper filled the air. Moments later, Kirsty and Brian were gone. Amelia found herself stood between Kevin and Helen, who was still clutching the bouquet.

"Who's the lucky fella?" Kevin teased her.

Helen's normally pale features flushed bright red. She was tongue tied. As the crowd dispersed to their cars, Amelia rescued her.

"Ignore Kevin. He's got a warped sense of humour."

"I know," Helen told her. "He's in my year at school."

"Who are you calling warped?" Kevin complained. "Have you been sneaking a look at me in the changing room?"

Both girls laughed and the bridesmaid's face resumed its normal colour. Helen's parents called her.

"Come on. We've got to get to the reception before the crowd."

The reception was in a big, anonymous hotel in

the nearby new town. The meal was unexciting but at least they were given wine with it. Sensibly, all of the teenagers had been put on the same table. Helen, as a bridesmaid, sat on the long table facing the rest of the room. It looked like a dull place to be. Helen had no one but the groom's seven-year-old sister to talk to. She kept glancing at Amelia and Kevin's table, as though she would kill to be on it.

"Do you fancy a church wedding, Amelia?" Steve Hooper asked, smarmily.

"She doesn't," Kevin piped up, before Amelia had time to think of a smart reply. "Amelia's going to have a supermarket wedding. That way, the guests can attend the wedding and buy the presents at the same time."

Steve frowned like he wanted to hit Kevin. Amelia burst into a fit of hysterical giggles. She wasn't sure whether she was laughing because of Kevin's daft joke or because of the wine, beginning to go to her head. But the joke had just the right effect. Steve didn't try and speak to her again for the rest of the meal.

The speeches, mercifully, were short. After coffee, everyone was ushered out of the dining room, so that it could be cleared and a dance floor set up for later. Amelia made her way to one of the Ladies' rooms, so that she could freshen up, and change her formal long skirt for baggy silk leggings. Helen was already in the room, changing.

"Boy, am I glad to get out of that dress," she told Amelia, with relief. "It made me look about *thirty*."

"You looked good in it," Amelia said, unconvincingly.

"*You* might have looked good in it," Helen told her. "You'd look great in a black plastic bin bag. But I looked like a stick insect in a maternity dress."

Amelia laughed. Then, while Helen was otherwise occupied, she examined herself in the mirror. People went on about Amelia's looks. They said she ought to be a model when she left school. It was true that she had the right figure for the job, and she was showing it off this evening. However, Amelia was conscious of her imperfections. She wasn't tall enough, for a start. Yes, her hair was dark and thick and long. It did more or less anything she wanted it to. But it wasn't quite jet black, unless she dyed it, which she was reluctant to do. She had rich brown eyes, but her brows were just a little too thick, so she had to pluck them very carefully. Some people called the mole to the right of her wide lips a beauty spot, but Amelia thought of it as a gaping flaw. She hated the tiny grey hair which grew out of it. And her teeth, finally: they were white and perfectly regular — two years of braces had seen to that — but they jutted out. Only slightly, but some people noticed it when she laughed.

"How do I look?"

Helen had changed into black jeans and a white, satin top which suited her.

"You look great," Amelia told her, sincerely this time. "I'm sure that you'll get him. Whoever he is."

Helen smiled bashfully. "I don't think he even notices me."

"Who?"

"Kevin."

"Kevin *Atkinson*?"

"Who else?"

It was hard to think of young Kevin as anyone's boyfriend. Amelia thought of Kevin more as her little brother. Which he was, in a way. Like her, he was an only child. Near neighbours, they had played together for years. Or, rather, Kevin had let Amelia boss him around in whatever make-believe game she thought of that day.

"I'm not sure if Kevin's ready for girlfriends yet," Amelia told Helen, tactfully. "He can be a bit immature."

"*All* boys are immature," Helen said. "I think he's gorgeous."

A large woman in her fifties came into the room and dumped a gargantuan make-up bag above the sink. It was time to go. Amelia finished touching up her lipstick and muttered a hurried 'good luck' to Helen as they returned to the reception.

Amelia queued at the bar. While she was waiting she tried to picture Kevin with Helen. If Helen had been a friend of hers, Amelia would have offered advice on how to attract Kevin. She might even have offered to try and steer Kevin in Helen's direction. But she hadn't offered. Why? It wasn't because Amelia hardly knew Helen. It must be for the opposite reason. She knew Kevin too well. You didn't help your girlfriends to get off with your little brother. Even if he wasn't really your brother.

The first drink at the bar was free. Amelia got herself a bitter lemon and looked around her. Quite a lot of people were coming for the evening only, but it wasn't seven yet, so it was all the same faces as before. Music pumped loudly from the ballroom. Amelia decided to see what was going on. The tables from earlier on had been pushed together at one end of the hall, and half of the carpet had been rolled away, revealing a good-sized dance floor. Small groups of people were scattered around the badly-lit room. Four children were standing in the middle of the dance floor, doing the Birdy song. She noticed a shadow in the back right-hand corner of the room. The shadow began to wave. Amelia walked over and joined Kevin.

"Welcome to the hippest club in town."

Kevin winked at her. He'd taken off his jacket. His only other concession to the more casual nature of the evening had been to loosen his jazzy tie and undo one button of his pink cotton shirt.

"Want to dance?" he asked.

Amelia had to look to the dance floor and back before she realized that Kevin was joking. As they laughed, she saw Helen peering around the entrance where she had stood moments before. Amelia beckoned her over.

"Ask Helen later," Amelia told him. "I'm sure she'll say yes."

There, Amelia thought. I've done her a favour. Kevin said nothing. As Helen sat down to join them, he hardly acknowledged her. Instead, he launched into one of his comic routines.

"Is he like this in school?" Amelia asked Helen.

Though Amelia attended the same school as Kevin, she didn't see much of him there, except on the bus: the years didn't mix a lot.

"It depends on the audience," Helen replied.

Abruptly, Kevin shut up. A dark look crossed his face. Amelia thought that she or Helen had offended him somehow. But then she felt a kiss landing on her bare shoulders, and she understood. Her boyfriend, Rick Jones, leant over her, and, this time, Amelia kissed him full on the lips. Then Rick took off his black leather jacket. He draped it across the chair on one side of Amelia and put his motorbike helmet next to it. Finally, he sat down on the other side of her.

"You know Kevin," Amelia said, formally.

"I've seen him around."

Rick nodded and Kevin nodded back.

"And this is Helen."

"Hello."

Rick saw that something more than a nod was required.

"Nice to meet you," he said, begrudgingly.

To fill the awkward silence, Amelia launched into a long monologue about the wedding, making it sound like it was a bigger deal to her than it actually had been. Then she asked Rick about his day. Rick told her about a run he'd been on to the sea-side with a group of his friends.

"They wanted me to – you know – stay and do the clubs tonight, but I told them I'd promised you . . ."

"I'm glad you came."

Amelia put her arm around Rick's shoulder and gave him another long kiss. Soon, she would have been going out with Rick for three months, longer than she'd been with any boy before. All Amelia's friends envied her. They wanted a lean, fit, handsome biker from the Sixth-Form College for themselves. Rick had hazel eyes and thick, curly fair hair. Amelia was the first girl he'd seriously dated. And she meant to hang onto him.

When they'd finished kissing, Amelia was aware that Kevin and Helen were embarrassed.

"Sorry," Amelia said. "You know how it is. We missed each other."

"Oh, stop showing off, Amelia," Kevin snapped.

Amelia bit her lip. She was hurt. It was ages since Kevin had been rude to her: not since he was ten and she'd gone off to secondary school and stopped playing with him. The conversation failed to flow. Rick never said a lot, but tonight he was particularly monosyllabic. Helen tried to get Kevin to tell some stories about school, but he'd lost the wit he had had earlier. The weight of conversation fell on Amelia, who soon ran out of things to say. She wished that more people would arrive. It was a merciful release when the Disc Jockey announced the buffet.

When most people had finished eating, they stopped playing novelty records and the music got more serious. The DJ insisted on getting the bride and groom out onto the floor for *their* song. This turned out to be "The Time of Our Lives", which Amelia hated. But then, as everyone began to dance, he played an old Jackson Five song.

"Come on, everybody."

Amelia smiled at the younger couple, then dragged the reluctant Rick onto the dance floor.

11

Kevin and Helen, Amelia noticed, as she melted into Rick's arms, were still sitting down, arms folded. Kevin hadn't taken the hint. Well, what more could she have done? As the song ended, Rick drew Amelia even closer and kissed her full on the mouth. The mirrored ball above them began to sparkle and spin. The evening was beginning properly now. At last Amelia could relax and enjoy herself. Rick began to whisper softly in her ear. Sometimes, when you least expected it, he could be very romantic.

"I'll tell you what," he said, softly. "Let's get out of this dump before I die of boredom."

September

2

Kevin sat in the assembly hall, getting bored. His Head of Year, Mrs Turner, was droning on about the school year which began that day.

"Now you're in the Fourth Year. It's your tenth year of school education, but the first one where you'll be studying for exams which really matter, GCSEs. This is what the last nine years have been leading up to . . ."

Kevin let his eyes wander. Pete Bullock, on the row in front of him, had his football tucked under his chair, so there'd be a game on at lunchtime. On the next row, chubby Martyn Turner, his best mate, had promised to bring in the new Amiga magazine for Kevin to read.

Two places along from Martyn sat Helen Scott, who he'd had a couple of dances with on Saturday night. Kevin rather liked Helen, with her long, blonde hair and her slightly sappy smile. She was easy to get on with. But he hoped she didn't think he wanted to go out with her. He wasn't ready to have a girlfriend yet. Once you started getting into that stuff, life got too serious: that was what he and his mates reckoned.

"There will be many temptations outside school and, I warn you, as the months go by these will get harder, rather than easier, to deal with. . ."

On the other hand, Kevin thought, it was clear that Helen liked him, and she wasn't the sort of girl who'd mess you around. Kevin could do a lot worse.

But then there was Amelia.

Kevin couldn't see how any girl he might go out with could compare with Amelia Gorman. She'd been his best friend until he was ten and she moved on to Secondary school. They were still pretty close. If Kevin found it easy to get on with girls, which he did, it was because of Amelia. She often talked through her problems with him. Mainly, recently, they had been about boys. Their next conversation, he was sure, would be about boring Rick, last Saturday night. She and Rick had had some kind of row, Kevin was sure, which led to them leaving the reception early. Kevin hoped Amelia would drop Rick, with his leathers and his motorbike. Rick thought he was some kind of stud. He didn't really care about Amelia, Kevin reckoned. He was only after her for one thing.

Suddenly, Kevin was aware that his name had been called out. Helen Scott turned round and smiled at him, then stood up. Kevin realized that he'd been staring at the back of her head while he thought about Amelia. Helen would think . . .

oh, never mind what Helen thought. Kevin turned to Chris Monk, sitting next to him.

"I was miles away. What's that she's reading out?"

"English groups. You should be on your way to the classroom now."

Kevin picked up his bag and followed Helen out of the hall. She was waiting for him by the drinks machine.

"Who've we got?" he asked her.

"Mrs Baggeley."

Kevin nodded. He looked at the other kids walking towards the room – no one he was particularly friendly with. He was going to end up sitting next to Helen in the lesson, he could see. Well, there were worse fates.

"How was your day?"

Six-and-a-half hours later, Kevin was sitting next to Amelia on the bus going home.

"Could have been worse," Kevin told her. Baggeley for English. Spark for Maths. We had a good match at lunch. How was yours?"

Amelia turned up the corners of her mouth.

"The usual rubbish: lectures about overdue coursework, 'the most important year of your school career', etcetera, etcetera."

Amelia wasn't too keen on school, never had been. She wasn't too keen on school uniform either. At the moment she was wearing a blue denim jacket and a white blouse with a fancy squiggly bit of embroidery down the middle. She was also wearing discreet make-up and small golden hoops in each of her ears. School regulations said no make-up of any kind, no ear-rings – only studs in pierced ears, and plain clothes in black, white or grey. But Amelia was the sort of girl who teachers turned a blind eye for.

"Oh, there's Helen."

Amelia gave the younger girl a smile. Helen forced half a smile back, aimed more at Kevin than Amelia, then sat down at the other end of the bus, on her own. Kevin was surprised to see her there. She didn't usually sit on the top deck.

"I hope you danced with her on Saturday night," Amelia told Kevin sternly.

"Yeah. After you left."

"She likes you."

"I know."

Kevin felt embarrassed. If Amelia wasn't going to change the subject, he would.

"What happened with you and Rick then?"

It was Amelia's turn to look embarrassed.

"Oh, you know what Rick's like."

Kevin only knew what Amelia told him, which always seemed to come through rose-tinted spectacles. Amelia went on.

"He's not much of a dancer and I made him stay longer than he wanted. We ended up going back to my house."

Kevin nodded, sympathetically. Amelia clammed up. She wasn't going to tell Kevin about the tacky way her evening had ended. Rick had taken her home, early. Mum and Dad were still at the wedding reception. She and Rick went up to Amelia's bedroom. It was nice for about ten minutes, but then Rick had put on his hot and bothered act.

"We've been going out for three months. You know I'm serious about you!"

"If you're serious then you'll wait until I'm ready."

"What do you think I have been doing? Most blokes . . ."

"I don't *care* what most blokes would do. I want it to happen when it feels right, not just because we happen to have the house to ourselves . . ."

To make matters worse, before they could work out the argument, Mum and Dad's taxi arrived. Rick made a fast exit. He wasn't much good with parents. While Dad was out of the room, Mum made a pointed comment about Amelia's some-what discomposed state.

"I hope you know what you're doing, young lady. . ."

Amelia had said that she did, then hurried off to bed before the discussion got any heavier. Tonight Amelia would ring Rick up. He would mumble into the phone for a couple of minutes, then he'd say that he had an essay to do before college started tomorrow. She would tell him that she loved him and he would mutter something which sounded like "me, too" and then "see you on Saturday".

They usually went out twice a week, once to the pictures and once to a party or for drinks somewhere. Rick didn't like to commit himself more than that, and neither, said Amelia, did she. Sometimes, during the summer, they had seen each other five days a week, but things were bound to cool off now that school had started up. Rick took his 'A' levels this year, and Amelia her GCSEs.

"Penny for them."

Kevin was standing up. It was their stop.

"Sorry," Amelia said, "I was thinking about Rick."

She followed him down the steps to the bottom of the bus. As Kevin descended the stairs he nodded at Helen Scott, who smiled shyly back. He and Amelia walked to the end of Amelia's driveway together, in silence. Now it was Kevin who seemed preoccupied.

"See you tomorrow then," Amelia told Kevin.

"Yeah. Bye."

Kevin trudged off without another word. He lived in a more modest house two streets away. Amelia wondered what was wrong with him. It wasn't like Kevin to be depressed.

An hour later, Kevin was sitting alone in his bedroom, thinking. Jealousy. That was what he'd felt. Kevin hated to think of Amelia getting all soppy about a jerk like Rick Jones. Yet, the boyfriends she'd had before hadn't bothered him much. What right did Kevin have to be jealous of Rick Jones? It wasn't as though Kevin went out with Amelia, too, or ever could be her boyfriend. Kevin was just a friend, who she trusted with her problems. Maybe it *was* time for him to have a girlfriend, no matter what his mates said. Kevin had noticed the way Helen looked at him on the bus today. That had been jealousy, too. He didn't want Helen to get the wrong idea about him and Amelia. Kevin had enjoyed sitting next to Helen in English today. She'd been on about a new Tom Cruise film which had just opened. Maybe . . .

Kevin went down to the hall and looked up "Scott" in the phone book. There were hundreds of them. But only one, he eventually discovered, in Coddington. It would be better, he knew, to ask her out face to face. But you never knew who else would be around, and some things were so much easier on the phone.

"555 1926."

"Eh, hello. Is Helen there, please?"

"Yes, who's calling?"

"It's . . . um, Kevin Atkinson."

"Oh, hello Kevin." The suspicious tone in Helen's mum's voice disappeared. "I'll just get her for you."

Kevin heard distant footsteps, a knocking, then the sound of feet hurrying down the stairs. He ought to have rehearsed what he was going to say to her.

"Kevin?"

"Hi."

Silence. How do you start a conversation like this?

"Did you want something?"

Her voice was reassuringly gentle, but Kevin still bottled it.

"That English homework. It's not due for tomorrow, is it?"

"We don't have English again until Monday. You're a real dreamer, aren't you, Kevin? Didn't you copy out your new timetable?"

"Yeah. But I can't remember where I put it," Kevin lied. "It was all right in English today," he went on. "She's not such an old bag, really."

"She will be, if you don't hand your homework in on time," Helen said. "Believe me. I had her last year."

"Oh. Right."

He wondered how many boys had asked Helen out before. What words did they use?

"Was there something else?"

"Yeah." Kevin took a deep breath. "In case I don't run into you tomorrow." – Which was practically impossible, since they took the same bus home – "I wondered if you wanted to go to the pictures on Saturday. That film you were on about."

There was a pause. She's going to turn me down, Kevin thought. I've read this all wrong.

"I didn't hint that strongly, did I?" Helen said, her voice going slightly giggly. "I mean, was I being really obvious?"

"No, no. I just thought we might, you know . . ."

"OK," she said. "So you'll come round and collect me, about seven then?"

"Fine. Seven."

"See you at school tomorrow then."

"Yeah. See you. Bye."

Kevin put the phone down. That was done. He'd made his first date. It felt good. He wanted to tell somebody about it. Kevin felt like ringing up Amelia. Almost. She'd be pleased for him, but telling her could wait. He'd see how it went first. Already, his brain was rushing with details. There were important things to work out. Like,

who paid? And, did that include the bus fare?
Little things, but he needed to know them if the
date was going to be a success.

3

Amelia's friends Gilli and Karen were nick-named "Little and Large". This was because Gilli was five feet ten and built like a champion hockey player, while Karen was a foot smaller, with a slight figure. If Amelia were to associate Karen with a game, it would be a TV quiz show. She always seemed to be either concentrating or about to burst into laughter. Gilli's every expression and attitude was more casual. She was easily bored, like Amelia.

Karen and Gilli were an unlikely couple to be best friends, but they were, and they were also the girls with whom Amelia got on best in school. Neither of them had boyfriends, but they were very happy to discuss her relationship with Rick.

"So you're seeing him tomorrow night?" Gilli asked.

"Yes. His parents are out and he wanted me to go round his place and watch a video, but I knew how that would end up so I insisted we go to see a film instead."

"A video sounds cosier," Karen murmured.

"It can get too cosy," Amelia complained. "You know, I really love Rick and all that, but I think if I don't sleep with him pretty soon he's going to dump me."

"If he dumps you because of that, he can't really love you, can he?" Gilli said.

Amelia thought for a moment.

"But you know how he gets around that. 'If you don't want to do it with me, then you can't really love me.' I never know how to reply."

Gilli shrugged.

"Maybe he's right. But if you're not ready, you're not ready. Maybe it's because you don't love him enough. Or maybe it's because you don't feel old enough. No one should make you do things you don't want to do."

"Sometimes I want to," Amelia said. "But I want to be sure."

Karen had different ideas.

"You're just afraid, that's all. I think Gilli's wrong. You've been with Rick for ages. He loves you and you love him. Once you've slept with him a couple of times you'll wonder why you haven't been doing it for months."

That was Karen, hard-headed as ever. Gilli teased her.

"Just listen to the voice of experience. If Amelia doesn't feel right about it, she shouldn't do it. What's the rush? She's got the rest of her life to fathom the mysteries of the orgasm!"

Amelia laughed. But Karen didn't let up.

"Rick's gorgeous. If you keep holding out on him he'll think you're being unfair. Because you are. It's only natural for guys his age . . ."

"Oh, come on!" Gilli interrupted. "Don't give us that 'boys and their urges' line. That's about as credible as 'wait until you're married'."

"That's exactly what my parents say," Karen told them. "'We waited, and it worked for us. So why shouldn't you?' Come on, get a life!"

"I still don't know what to do," Amelia said. "What if he starts cooling off?"

Gilli shook her head.

"It's more likely to work the other way. Go to bed with him and then he'll cool off, start to treat you like dirt."

"Rick's not like that."

Gilli looked her straight in the eye. "Are you *sure*?"

Amelia wasn't sure, really. Rick could be so quiet and moody with her. When he was with his mates, playing pool, or swapping stories down the pub, he was a different person: loud, aggressive even. When he was with her, he never seemed to have opinions about things. For instance, he always let her choose what film they went to. The result was that, half the time, she chose the picture she thought he most wanted to see. Often, she got it wrong, and neither of them enjoyed themselves. She said some of this to Karen and Gilli.

"All blokes are like that," Karen said.

"To some extent," Gilli qualified. "You have to put up with it."

"Kevin's not like that," Amelia retorted. "He's got lots of opinions and he talks about his feelings sometimes."

"But Kevin's not your *boyfriend*," Gilli told her. "And he's never likely to be. If he *was*, he'd act differently towards you. You're always saying that you've got a kind of brother/sister relationship with him."

"It's not like my relationship with my little brother," Karen chirped in. "I can't stand him. Though maybe if he was really good looking, like Kevin . . ."

"You fancy *Kevin*?" Gilli acted shocked. "Diddy Kevin?"

"He's tall enough for me," Karen replied, in a huff. "Why not?"

"Cradle snatcher!" Gilli teased.

Karen laughed. Amelia laughed too, though she wasn't sure that the joke was really funny.

The film was pretty stupid. Kevin wasn't sure which was the worst – the plot or the American actors' Irish accents. But Helen seemed to enjoy it. She looked great – a white cotton top and grey jeans – dead simple and stylish. During the film, Kevin held Helen's hand. He wasn't sure if he was meant to do more. If there had been scary moments, he might have put his arm around her, the way Amelia used to make him do when they watched videos together as kids. But it wasn't that kind of film.

"What did you think of it?" Kevin asked Helen as they came out into the foyer.

"Pretty good," Helen said. "You didn't enjoy it, did you?"

"How could you tell?"

"You kept shifting in your chair, the way you do in boring assemblies."

"How do you know how I act when I'm bored in assembly?"

Helen gave him a secretive smile.

"I've been watching you for a while, Kevin Atkinson."

Kevin smiled back and put his arm round her shoulder. It was easy really, no big deal. Helen slid her arm round his waist and the next thing you knew they were kissing. Not a big kiss. More a sort of soft meeting of the lips. But it was a first kiss, and it was over with. Now he could kiss her again when he was ready without having to get all worried about it. Kevin was so busy trying to decide whether to kiss Helen again straightaway that he didn't notice Amelia and Rick until they were right in front of him.

"Hi," Helen said. "What film have you been to see?"

Rick nodded. Amelia, looking flustered, replied. "'Wild Love'. It was quite good. Which did you go to?"

Kevin told her.

"It was quite good too," he lied.

It seemed important not to acknowledge that he hadn't had a perfect time on his first date.

"Where are you going now?" Amelia asked next.

"Dunno."

Kevin turned to Helen. "You want to go for a burger or something before we go home?"

"Sure. Why not?"

"You've only got twenty minutes before the last bus," Amelia said, sounding like his mother.

"And we've only got ten before last orders," Rick grumbled. "Come on."

He yanked Amelia's arm and they were gone.

Kevin and Helen turned up the hill towards Wimpy's. But then Helen stopped. "I'm not really hungry," she said. "Are you? There's always drunks on the last bus," she went on. "Let's get the one before. It'll be quieter. You could come back for a coffee."

"Yeah. Fine."

There was hardly anybody on the bus. Kevin and Helen sat behind a couple of girls dressed up to the nines. They'd either been dumped by their boyfriends or had given up on finding one and were settling for the midnight movie instead. On the other side was a middle-aged couple who'd probably been to the pictures too.

Kevin and Helen sat on the back seat. Once the bus started, Kevin kissed Helen – properly this time, a real kiss, like the one he'd watched Amelia giving Rick last Saturday night. It felt good, if a little weird. It was like discovering part of yourself you'd always known was there, but hadn't really thought about. The kiss was soft, and exciting and, in a nice sort of way, disturbing. Kevin couldn't work out what the rules for kissing were. Helen closed her eyes, so he closed his. How long was it meant to go on for? After a minute or two, Helen pulled gently away. Did that mean that the girl decided when it was over?

"That was nice," she said.

"Very nice."

"Let's do it again."

They did, and Helen pulled him closer this time, so that he could feel her chest pressing against his. It was a brilliant feeling. Kevin wanted it to last forever. Helen clung to him tightly. It was great, knowing that she felt the same way. He'd never guessed that a girl would feel this good. Time seemed to disappear. Before he knew it, the twenty-minute ride to Coddington was over. Kevin only just managed to ring the bell to stop the bus in time. Helen's house was a short walk from the bus stop. It was a small semi, like Kevin's parents', with only the tiniest patch of grass at the front. There was nowhere to hide and carry on what they'd started on the bus.

"Are you coming in?"

"Dunno."

Kevin knew Helen's parents by sight. He said hello to them in the street. But he wasn't sure how to adapt to his new role as their daughter's boyfriend.

"What are they like when you bring a boy home?"

Helen gave him a funny look. "How would I know? You're the first one."

Kevin ground his hands together. "I think I'm going to leave it for another time."

A light came on in the hall. "It's OK," Helen said. "You'd better go then. I'll see you on Monday. G'night."

She put her arms around his neck and gave him a peck on the lips. From inside the hallway, her mum's voice called, "Helen, is that you?" Kevin smiled and hurried back up the street before the door opened.

It was a fair walk from Helen's to his house, but Kevin didn't mind, even when it began to rain. He was walking on air. When Kevin was nearly home, he passed Amelia's house. The last bus had come now, she should be home. But there was no light on in her bedroom. She must have gone back to Rick's. Or maybe they'd stayed in town after the bus. Maybe Rick 'last orders' Jones could afford a taxi home. His parents lived in a house even bigger than Amelia's, on the outskirts of the village. Money went after money, Kevin knew. That was the way the world went.

"How did it go with Helen?" Mum wanted to know as soon as he got in.

"Brilliant."

"She seems like a nice girl."

"Yeah. She is."

"So be sure you treat her like one, won't you?"

"*Yes, Mum.*"

Kevin smiled and said good-night. In his bedroom, he switched on his video console, but, for once, he didn't feel like playing a game. In bed, he went over the evening with Helen in his mind. He could hardly remember what they'd talked about. He seemed to have talked less than usual. But then, you couldn't talk when you were kissing. The other thing that stuck in Kevin's mind was bumping into Amelia with Rick – the funny look she'd given him. You'd think that she wasn't the one who'd encouraged him to chat up Helen in the first place. Kevin and Helen were far better suited than Amelia and Rick, in Kevin's opinion. But that wasn't saying a lot. He'd known Amelia so long, and he thought so much of her – it was hard to think of any guy who'd be good enough for her.

Kevin went to bed. He had to be up before seven

31

to do his paper round. It was a funny feeling, falling asleep for the first time knowing that he had a girlfriend. What was he supposed to do next? Where did he go from here? Kevin hadn't the slightest idea.

4

"What's wrong with you?"

Rick broke away from Amelia and changed the tape in the machine. The music went from romantic soul to heavy metal. Amelia got the message.

"I don't know," she said. "It's just. . .I've noticed recently. . .we hardly talk to each other about things."

"What things?"

Rick was losing patience with her.

"Oh, I dunno. Feelings. Opinions. What you thought about the film tonight, for instance. You hardly said a word in the pub, just stared into your drink."

"There was nothing *to* think. It was just slam-bang-crash action. It wasn't supposed to make you *think*."

"Why did we go to it then?"

"Don't ask me. It was your idea."

Amelia stood up. She'd had enough.

"It's late. I'm tired. I'm going to call a taxi."

Rick stood too. He had a fierce expression on his face.

"No. Wait." He spoke loudly, to be heard over the music. "We haven't finished talking."

"We haven't started," Amelia snapped back.

The loud guitars and drums from the hi-fi were giving Amelia a headache. The singer had a terrible voice. She could hear some of the words and they were really sexist. Women in songs like this were objects – adored one minute, there to be used and abused the next. If Amelia asked Rick why he liked them, he would say that the words were meant to be funny and no one listened to them, anyway. Amelia hoped he was fooling himself, because he wasn't fooling her.

"I'm going."

Amelia picked up her woollen jacket and put it on. Rick grabbed her shoulder. He was getting ugly now.

"Everyone warned me when I started going out with you. They said you'd mess me around, that you always dropped your boyfriends when they started getting serious. You're frigid, you know that?"

"Oh yeah," said Amelia, sarcastically. "That's me. The Ice Queen."

Rick acted like he hadn't even heard her. "You only want a boyfriend to show off to your friends. You chose me because I look old and I've got a bike. You tell me I've got nothing interesting to say, but it's you who's not interested."

"That's not true."

Amelia was getting angry, too, and a little scared. This was a side of Rick she hadn't seen. She spoke assertively.

"If you really think that about me, maybe we

ought to pack it in. Now I'm going to call a taxi."

Rick didn't let go.

"I want you to stay. I want to be with you!"

"And I want to go home!"

Amelia was on the verge of tears.

"Oh, turn that horrible music off!"

Rick did as she asked. Amelia sat down.

"I'm confused," she told him. "I don't know what I want. Sometimes we seem so close. Other times you seem like a stranger."

Rick still looked hurt.

"It's not always easy going out with you," he said. "I didn't mean to lose my temper, but. . ."

For a moment, Amelia was tempted to stay. Rick could be so nice when he was making up. But she didn't want to give in so easily, to show weakness. . .

"Let's just leave it for a week," Amelia said. "Not see each other. Then we can talk properly. I don't want it to end like this."

Rick stared at her. The anger seemed to be fading from his face. Amelia put her arms round his waist and hugged him. She could feel the tension in his body.

"I'll drive you home," he said.

"No," Amelia told him. "You've been drinking. I'll get a taxi."

She'd promised her parents when she started going out with Rick – no riding on his motorbike when they were drinking alcohol. She was allowed to drink a little and they trusted her to drink sensibly. But that trust didn't extend to the boys she dated. Tonight, she and Rick had caught the bus into the new town and back.

"I had two-and-a-half pints nearly an hour ago," Rick told her. "It's out of my system now."

"Yes, but, still . . ."

Rick spoke gently. "I want to take you home. When you're thinking about me this week, I want you to remember what it's like, riding with me on the bike."

Amelia smiled reluctantly. "All right. But don't go right up to my house. I don't want Mum and Dad to hear."

Downstairs, she put on Rick's spare helmet. They went outside. Rick started the bike and she got onto it, her arms clinging tightly around his chest. They set off into the pale, moonlit night. Rick lived just off the main road on the outskirts of the village, nearly two miles from Amelia's house. They turned onto the main road and Rick opened up the throttle.

"Not too fast," Amelia shouted, over the engine noise.

But, if Rick heard, he ignored her. Now he speeded up along the dual carriageway. It was an exhilarating feeling, but scary too. Amelia could see the the numbers zooming up on the speedometer: 50, 60, 70, 75. . . Amelia screamed. "Slow down!"

If he could hear her, this time Rick's only response was to go faster. He would have to brake soon though, when they turned off into Coddington. Rick took the corner way too fast. Amelia, holding on for dear life, was sure that they were going to come off. But they didn't. The village shops shot by. Rick was breaking the speed limit. He was still angry. He was showing off. There was bound to be a police car, any second now.

But there wasn't. Before she realized where they were, Rick was parking outside Amelia's driveway. She'd wanted him to drop her off on the road before, so that Mum and Dad wouldn't hear him. But right now she was too relieved to complain. Amelia got off the bike and handed Rick his helmet.

"Good-night."

Rick lifted off his helmet. His hair was ruffled and lit up by the moon, shining from behind. He'd never looked more handsome. "I love you," he said.

Amelia stared at him for a moment. Then, without saying anything, she turned and walked down the driveway to the front door. As she turned the key in the lock she heard Rick rev his motorbike loudly, then ride off. The clock in the hall said one o'clock. Amelia heard a bedroom door opening. A moment later, Mum was standing at the top of the stairs, in her dressing gown.

"Amelia! I thought we told you not to let Rick . . ."

"Forget it," Amelia interrupted. "I won't be seeing him again."

"Oh."

Mum came downstairs.

"Did you argue about something?"

She pulled a tissue out of her dressing gown pocket and handed it to Amelia. Amelia took it. It was only then that she realized that she was crying.

"Not really." Amelia tried to think. "I'm not quite sure how it happened, to be honest."

"But he broke off with you?"

Mum's voice was full of concern.

"No. I broke off with him. Or, at least, I'm going to."

"Then you shouldn't be so upset, should you?"

Amelia started crying again. "It's hard to explain. But I think . . . if I don't finish with him, then he'll finish with me. Maybe not next week, but next month, or the one after."

Mum put her arm round Amelia's shoulder. "That doesn't make a whole lot of sense. Wait there."

Mum went to the kitchen and made Amelia some hot chocolate, her favourite late night comfort drink. When she came back, Amelia had stopped crying.

"Has he been cooling off on you?" Mum asked.

"Yes. No. Maybe. I'm not sure if I'd know the signs."

Mum shook her head. "Oh, I'm sure you'd know the signs, Amelia. Is there another boy?"

Amelia was affronted.

"No! Of course not! What do you think I am?"

"I think you're a girl not yet sixteen who doesn't know what she wants."

Amelia nodded. "Yes. I guess that about sums it up."

"Go to bed, darling. Things will seem clearer in the morning."

Amelia did as her mum suggested. She took her drink to bed with her. But she couldn't sleep. Her mind was a mess. She kept picturing Rick, his hair all mussed up in the moonlight, saying "I love you." But another picture kept recurring just as strongly, though there was no real reason for it to. Amelia kept remembering Kevin walking into the Odeon foyer with his arm wrapped around Helen Scott. She remembered the tender way Kevin had kissed Helen, then looked over and, seeing Amelia, had smiled. Amelia wasn't sure how she'd reacted. But she'd felt then like someone had taken a knife and stabbed her deep in the heart, then twisted it. What was more, she still felt that way now.

"So what did you do last night then?"

It was Sunday afternoon. Kevin had gone round to his friend Martyn's to watch the Premier division match on satellite TV.

"Went to the pictures."

"On your own?"

Martyn wasn't offended. He thought that the cinema was a waste of money. He preferred watching films on video.

"No. I went with Helen Scott."

Martyn raised both eyebrows in a deliberately silly expression.

"*Helen Scott*! From our year?"

"That's the one."

Martyn frowned. "You're a slippery customer sometimes, Kev. I thought you said. . ."

Kevin shrugged. "You've got to start going out with girls sometime, haven't you?"

Martyn didn't look convinced. "Yeah, but Helen. . . I mean, she's all right, but I thought the only girl you were interested in was Amelia Gorman."

Kevin smiled. "That's right. Her and Madonna. But they're both a bit out of my league, aren't they?"

Martyn shook his head. "I dunno. I've heard Madonna prefers younger men. . ."

They both laughed, and the match started. Kevin was glad that Martyn had taken the news about Helen so lightly. He was bound to get some ribbing when word got out at school, but he could handle that. He'd wanted Martyn to hear it from him first. Well, Martyn and Amelia. Amelia, however, had seen for herself. Kevin supposed she was pleased. Hadn't she sort of tried to set him up with Helen, at the wedding last week? All the same, he'd felt funny seeing her in the Odeon last night. And she'd given him the oddest look, now he thought about it. Like she'd seen a ghost.

Normally, he would have called in on Amelia on the way back from Martyn's. They often dropped in on each other. Kevin went round to Amelia's rather more often, because it was a bigger house. Today, though, he felt funny about it for some reason. She would expect him to tell her all about his night with Helen, but Kevin didn't feel like it, yet. Nor did he want to hear any more about her relationship with Rick Jones. But if he didn't show up at all over the weekend, Amelia might think there was something wrong. OK then. Let her come and see him. Otherwise, they'd catch the bus together after school, as normal. He'd see her then.

"Brilliant goal!"

"Wha . . ."

Kevin blinked at the screen and waited for the replay. Martyn gave him a condescending look. "You missed it, didn't you?"

Kevin nodded.

"What's happening to you? One date with a girl and you go all distracted! I don't see how you can suddenly go all soppy over Helen Scott. You've known her since you were in the Infants."

"Nah, it's not that. It's just. . .well, things start getting complicated."

Martyn smiled wryly. "We always said that, didn't we? Once you start going out with girls, your life isn't your own. Your mates take second place. You always said you wouldn't let it happen, Kev. No complications."

Kevin punched his friend in his large, flabby stomach.

"You're right. No complications."

They returned to watching the match. No complications, thought Kevin. An easy thing to say. But what did you do if your feelings were complicated?

5

Home time. Late out of Maths, Amelia made the bus with a minute to spare. Mondays were always bad but this one seemed to have lasted forever. All day Amelia had been feeling guilty about the way she'd treated Rick on Saturday night. After all, *he* hadn't been any different. It was her. And, all day, she had been waiting for a chance to talk to Kevin.

Amelia climbed the stairs. The top deck of the bus was much noisier than the lower one, which meant that it was possible to have a private conversation. Usually, Kevin managed to save a place for Amelia near the front of the bus. Today, though, she saw that all the seats there were full. They would be forced to sit at the back, where all the smokers hung out. Where was Kevin? He must have been kept behind for missing work, like her. Luckily, there was, she saw, still one double seat free. Then she noticed him. Kevin was sitting in the second row from the front. He was glancing back towards her. Amelia watched as he turned down his lips in what she supposed was meant to be an apologetic smile. But Amelia could see what he was really feeling – embarrassment. Kevin was sitting next to Helen Scott.

Amelia sat down in the free seat near the back of the bus. She was fuming, though she knew she had no right to be annoyed. It was a lousy ending to a lousy day. But what should she have expected? Now that Kevin had a girlfriend, of course he would sit next to her on the bus. Amelia couldn't have felt worse. She had managed to lose her boyfriend and her best friend in the same weekend.

"This seat free?"

Amelia nodded reluctantly. The speaker was Dean Gates, who was in her form. Dean was a heavily-built, badly-dressed boy who had had a crush on Amelia for about a year, though he'd never worked up the nerve to ask her out. Amelia was always polite to Dean. This wasn't because she liked him. It was because she was a little afraid of him. Giving boys the brush-off wasn't easy at the best of times. And Dean wasn't the sort of boy who took a hint. Amelia would have to make her dislike really obvious, which she wasn't prepared to do.

"Not with your little boyfriend today?" Dean asked, sarcastically.

"Kevin's not my boyfriend. In fact, he's sitting with his girlfriend, at the front."

"Aaaah! Atkinson's got a girlfriend!" Dean called out, in a loud, yobbish voice.

Amelia squirmed for Kevin. It wasn't like her to open her mouth without thinking. At the front, of the bus, Kevin didn't turn round but his hair seemed to bristle.

"So, you're still seeing that bloke who used to come here, that Rick?" Dean asked her.

Amelia fibbed. "Yes."

"What's he doing this year, 'A' levels?"

She nodded. Dean continued to pry.

"And then he'll be gone to university, or wherever?"

"I guess."

Amelia saw where this was leading.

"And what about you? Are you going to do 'A' levels and all that?"

Dean knew that she hated school, like he did, and would get out at the earliest opportunity.

"No," she told him. "I'm going to go away with Rick and live with him."

Dean didn't try to hide his surprise. "Gah, really?"

"That's right. I'm going to get work as a model, or, if there isn't any, as a stripper, to support us — 'cos you know that students can't afford to live on their grants any more."

Even thick Dean could see that Amelia was being sarcastic. He shut up for the rest of the journey, not even saying goodbye when he got up to go, three stops before Amelia. As he walked off, shoulders hunched, Amelia felt guilty about humiliating him. He meant no real harm.

Amelia was getting off the bus when Kevin scrambled down the stairs and joined her. At least he hadn't gone home with Helen, too.

"You didn't mind me not sitting with you?" he asked, tentatively, when they were on the

44

path on their own. "I hoped you'd understand."

"'S all right," she said.

They began to walk in the direction of Amelia's house.

"Thought you might come round yesterday," he went on.

"I thought *you* might."

Kevin paused. "You're not mad at me, are you?"

"No, why should I be? It's just . . ."

She might as well tell him.

"I finished with Rick on Saturday night and I'm a bit upset about it."

"I didn't. . .you, you should have called. Amelia . . ."

Spontaneously, Kevin put his arm around Amelia and gave her a cuddle. He couldn't stand Rick, but knew better than to rub it in when she was hurt so badly.

"You want to talk about it?"

Amelia had let her head droop so that hair covered her face.

"Yeah. I guess."

Amelia's parents were both still at work. Amelia got Kevin and herself a coffee, then they took it up to her room. It was a nice room, twice the size of Kevin's, with a big bed and an old wicker chair, plants, cushions and some arty prints. Kevin noticed that the photo of Rick had gone from her mirror. He felt like gloating, but put on his most sympathetic voice.

"What happened?"

Amelia ignored the question.

"Did you have a good time with Helen on Saturday night?"

So maybe she didn't want to talk about Rick after all.

"Er, yeah. It was nice."

"What did you go and see?"

He was sure he'd told her on Saturday night, but he told her again, and gave a rough summary of the plot.

"So where are you taking her next?"

"Dunno."

Kevin had expected to be asked about the rest of the evening. Amelia never used to spare him the intimate details of her dates. But the questions stopped. There was an awkward silence.

"Like I said, I've packed Rick in," she told him, finally.

"You packed *him* in?"

"That's what I said."

"Why?"

Of course, it made sense that it was Amelia who'd dropped Rick. You couldn't imagine anyone packing her in. And she had given the push to her previous two boyfriends as well, when they started getting possessive. Kevin realized that she wasn't answering the question.

"I thought you were really keen on him," he said.

"I was. And he's still keen on me. But . . ."

Amelia was staring at him in a funny way.

"You know, sometimes, when I'm with a boy – not a boyfriend, but any boy, my age or older, I feel like a show-room dummy. Like the real me isn't there. They stare at my face and at my figure and they say how nice I look and they pretend not to be undressing me with their eyes . . . but they don't take any notice of me. They're not interested in who I am, what I think. You know what I mean?"

"I think so," Kevin said. "They're only interested in sex."

Amelia nodded. "And girls, too. They think that if you're good-looking, then you've got it made, and you should never complain about anything. Gilli and Karen, today, both told me I was mad to pack Rick in. Then Karen said, 'but I suppose you can afford to' – like the fact that I could find someone else easily was a consideration."

"Wasn't it?" Kevin asked.

Amelia shook her head vigorously.

"No! It's just . . . I didn't think Rick was interested in me, as a person. He was more interested in showing me off to his mates."

She paused. "But maybe I'm being unfair. Maybe all boys are like that."

Kevin finished his coffee. Amelia wondered what was going through his mind. Kevin hadn't said a word against Rick this afternoon, though he'd made it clear in the past that he didn't like him. Maybe he wasn't thinking about her and Rick at all. Maybe he was thinking about Helen.

Kevin stood up. "I've got to go," he said. "I'm going round to Helen's for my tea and I haven't told my mum yet."

"Ring her," Amelia said.

"I need to get changed, too."

"Oh. OK."

She let him go. Kevin gave her a big, boyish grin at the door.

"I'm sure you did the right thing about Rick,"

47

he told her. "You want to be with someone who likes you for what you are, who's easy to have a laugh with."

"I guess," Amelia said.

Kevin stood there, his white shirt flapping in the September breeze, his tie tucked in halfway down, the way some kids in the school's Fourth Year thought was stylish. He smiled again, then swung his bag over his shoulder and walked off down the driveway.

Amelia made herself another coffee and went back upstairs. She was stupid, being upset about Kevin having a girlfriend. After all, it was bound to happen. And it wasn't as though she could ever go out with a boy his age. If anything, she wanted a boy who was older, more mature, who knew that there was more to a relationship than sex. Tired, Amelia flopped on her bed and tried to doze. But she couldn't. She found herself thinking about Kevin going round to Helen's. If he hadn't been in such a hurry, Amelia would have warned him what he was in for.

Amelia had only once been round to a boy's house for a meal – Mike Todd, who she'd gone out with for three weeks when she was fourteen. The meal was excruciatingly embarrassing. Mike clammed up, leaving Amelia to do all the talking with his mum and older brother (Mike's father didn't live with them). Mrs Todd kept going on about what Amelia was going to do when she left school, and seemed shocked that she didn't want to go to university or be a nurse or something equally worthy.

"I'm sure that there are some very good jobs for

secretaries . . ." she had said, in a dubious tone.

Mike's older brother, Lee, told Amelia that she ought to be a model, she had the looks. A week later, when she'd chucked Mike, Lee rang her up and asked her out. When she turned him down, he seemed shocked. He'd managed to convince himself that Amelia had thrown over his brother purely because she wanted to go out with him, instead. Amelia had avoided every invitation to have a meal at a boyfriend's house since then. She wondered whether Kevin remembered her telling him the story, and whether, after tonight, he would feel the same. Probably he wouldn't. Kevin could charm anyone, if he chose to, Amelia knew. Including Amelia herself.

October

6

Kevin was sitting in the Year-Ten common room with Martyn and Chris. They were discussing how to survive for more than five minutes in a new computer game – *Debaser*. Martyn glanced over Kevin's shoulders.

"Watch up," he said. "It's your fan club."

Kevin looked round. Helen gave him a small wave. Kevin smiled back, but his spirits sank slightly. He and Helen had been going out for nearly a month now, and she was beginning to work her way into every part of his life. He would see Helen on the school bus, in lessons, at break times, on weekends and one or two weekday evenings as well. It was getting to be too much. Nevertheless, he got up and joined her. Martyn and Chris had no time for Helen. As far as they were concerned she was either soppy, boring or both. Sometimes, Kevin felt the same way.

"Hi," he said.

It was a clear, fresh October day. Kevin and Helen walked over the school fields to the mound where they could get a bit of privacy. Once they were out of sight of the school, Helen put her hand in his, and squeezed. Kevin squeezed back. At least Helen didn't do the really soppy stuff in front of his mates. The mound wasn't a terribly romantic place. You could hear the main road from there, a farmer's field away. Smokers used it a lot, and there were cigarette ends all over the ground. But at least you couldn't be seen. When they kissed, Kevin broke away first. Helen smiled.

"I was wondering," she said.

"Yeah?"

"What you wanted to do for your birthday. Have you got any plans?"

"It's not till the middle of November. That's ages away!"

She'd be talking about Christmas next.

"Yes, but I might need to make plans, save . . ."

"It's only my fifteenth birthday, OK? Don't make a big deal of it."

"But I want to," Helen simpered.

She kissed him again. Kevin held her close, but his mind wasn't on the kiss. He was thinking about Amelia. Her birthday was a fortnight before his, during half term. He always got her something nice, and especially wanted to this year, when she'd been so down recently. But going out with Helen had used up most of the money he got from his paper round. He would have to start saving for Amelia's present.

Helen broke away from the kiss. Kevin opened his eyes.

"I love you," she said, softly.

Kevin froze. He didn't say anything.

"What's wrong?"

This was getting too serious for him. "Nothing. It's just . . ."

Kevin avoided Helen's eyes. He felt his face reddening. He didn't know how to say what was on his mind.

"Tell me."

Kevin tried to look at Helen. Something had gone. She looked like the girl he remembered from the year before: long-haired, pale-faced, flat-chested, nothing special about her at all. Just another girl he'd known since the year dot.

"Tell me, Kevin."

He struggled for words. "I dunno. It's just . . . this is all getting a bit heavy for me. Maybe I'm not ready to have a girl . . . a *serious* girlfriend yet."

Suddenly the day felt very cold. Tears formed in Helen's eyes. Kevin felt terrible. He started to put his arms around her. Helen flinched and pulled away.

"*Don't* try to touch me!" she said. "And don't lie to me, either. I can see what's going on! You've never really been interested in me."

Kevin was confused. "What do you mean?"

"You only went out with me to make Amelia Gorman jealous!"

Kevin was flabbergasted. "That's not true."

Helen glared at him.

"No? That first night when you danced with me, it was only because Amelia Gorman had gone. And then, when you took me to the pictures, it was the same place she was at with her boyfriend."

"So?"

"So you were never interested in me. You just wanted to show her that you could go out with someone too!"

Kevin was shocked. "That's ridicu—"

"Don't try to deny it. You've been cooling off me ever since she split up with Rick Jones. I know you've been round to her house."

"She's a friend of mine. She's still upset about splitting up with her boyfriend. . ."

"*Three* weeks ago."

Helen sounded even more indignant. Kevin didn't reply. It seemed like anything he said would make things worse.

"I've seen the way you look at her," Helen went on. "She likes to keep you on a string, at her beck and call."

"That's rubbish," Kevin said, indignant himself now. "Anyway, I didn't see Amelia at all this weekend. I was with you most of the time. She's the one who should be offended!"

Helen slapped his face. Kevin was surprised how much it stung.

"Don't try and con me, Kevin Atkinson. And don't think you can finish with me, either. I'm finishing with you. There. You're free to go after your precious Amelia Gorman. See if she really wants you, or if she just enjoys stringing you along!"

Helen turned round and stalked off, tears streaming down her face. Kevin stood still for a moment, shocked. He didn't understand women. One minute Helen was being all clinging, and he was trying to cool things down. The next minute she was being all assertive and he was out on his ear. There were noises behind him. A group of Year Eleven kids stood there, cigarettes already lit. Kevin took off after Helen, hoping that none of the older kids had overheard their embarrassing conversation.

Amelia stood amongst the group of smokers, her mind a turmoil. None of the others seemed to have listened to the young couple's conversation. They were more interested in lighting up.

Amelia had only heard Kevin and Helen's last exchange, not what came before it. But that had been enough. Her mind burnt with what she'd heard. Helen had just chucked Kevin. Was she right? Was Kevin interested in Amelia as a girl-friend, not just as a friend? Or was she just another silly, jealous little girl? Amelia finished the cigarette. She was glad that Kevin hadn't seen her. This wasn't just because of the embar-rassing conversation, but because Amelia didn't want him to find out that she'd started smoking again. She only did it when she was depressed, but Kevin wouldn't take that as an excuse. He'd be really down on her if he knew. There was a conversation going on around her, but Amelia ignored it and walked back to the school build-ings. She passed the Fourth-Year common rooms. Kevin was nowhere to be seen. However, she could see Helen, sitting on a table, face red from crying, pouring her heart out to a couple of her friends. Probably, by tonight, Helen would have patched things up with Kevin. After all, they seemed to get on well together. Kevin didn't talk about Helen much. Amelia thought that this was because he didn't want to rub in that he had a girlfriend while she didn't have a boyfriend.

What Kevin didn't know was that several boys had asked her out since the news got around that she'd split up with Rick. Amelia had turned them all down. None of them seemed as nice as the boy she'd just lost. Maybe Kevin didn't talk about his girlfriend because he sensed how Helen made Amelia uneasy. She threatened their friendship. Or maybe Helen was right. Maybe Kevin didn't talk about Helen because he would really rather be going out with Amelia.

That afternoon, Amelia paid even less attention to her lessons than usual. Even in Drama, her favourite subject, she didn't get involved in the improvisation work. Mr Stimson, the teacher, tried to keep her behind.

"You've been getting more and more apathetic recently, Amelia. I'm concerned about you."

"I'm sorry, sir. I really need to catch the first bus. I'm meeting someone."

Mr Stimson looked hurt. Amelia felt guilty as she hurried off. But the feeling didn't last. Sometimes, she wondered whether male teachers would be so concerned about her if she was plain, like Helen Scott. There were times when Amelia caught teachers looking at her during lessons with the same guarded stare she got from men on the street and in pubs.

Amelia got onto the bus early and bagged a seat at the front, away from the smokers. Kevin arrived a few moments later. Without a word, he came and sat down next to her. Amelia knew better than to make any comment. The two of them sat in silence. Seconds after Kevin had sat down, Amelia saw Helen Scott in the mirror, climbing to the top of the stairs. She took one look at Kevin with Amelia and went back down again. Amelia had got there just in time. Kevin didn't say a word for the whole journey home – not a single comment or wisecrack. Only once they were off the bus did Amelia speak to him.

"Do you want to talk about it?"

Kevin stared at the pavement.

"There's nothing *to* talk about."

They walked on a bit. Amelia decided to try again.

"I saw Helen at lunchtime. She looked really upset."

"She's got no right to be upset!" Kevin snapped. "It was her who chucked me!"

Amelia put her arm around his shoulder, tenderly.

"Come on," she said. "Let's go and talk it through."

"I suppose."

His pride was hurt, Amelia realized, as she waited for the kettle to boil. That was why he found it hard to talk about. In a sense, though, what Helen did to him was the same as what she'd done to Rick. She'd dumped him because she was sure that he was about to dump her. Rick had rung just once since that last, painful motorbike ride. Amelia told her mum to tell him she was out. And she hadn't rung him. If Rick had called her a second time, pleaded, Amelia would probably have changed her mind and gone out with him again. It hurt that he hadn't. But she knew that he was proud and stubborn, so she wasn't exactly surprised. If Kevin called Helen, he would be able to turn her round, Amelia was sure of that. But she didn't tell him this, because she really didn't want him to. So, instead, she asked a question she already knew the answer to.

"Did Helen give a reason?"

Kevin felt really uncomfortable, but he was in Amelia's bedroom now, and he could hardly clam up on her.

"Nah. Well, it's embarrassing."

"Oh come on, Kevin. I've told you loads of embarrassing stories about me. We know each other well enough."

Kevin smiled ruefully. He wondered how embarrassed Amelia would be if he told her the whole thing.

"I guess. . . " he mumbled, then cleared his throat. "OK. First thing was, she told me that she loved me."

"And did you say it back?"

He shook his head. Amelia tut-tutted.

"Bad move. Girls expect you to say it. They might not expect you to mean it, but they definitely expect you to say it."

Kevin replied sarcastically. "I'll remember that. Girls prefer boys to lie. I like to learn from my mistakes."

"Come on," Amelia said. "What happened next?"

Kevin mumbled. "I was a bit freaked out. I told her I thought we were getting too serious, something like that."

"And?"

"Then she chucked me."

Amelia frowned. "Just like that? No other reason?"

Kevin took a deep breath. "You won't believe this," he said.

"Try me."

"OK."

Kevin looked at Amelia. She was still wearing her school clothes but it made no difference. She looked like girls you saw in magazines –not a year older than him, but five years . . . more. Helen's suggestion was absurd. He had to look to one side of Amelia before he could stutter her story out.

"What she said was – I'd never really been interested in her in the first place, that I'd gone out with her in order to make you jealous. And it worked, because you split up with Rick. So then it was only a matter of time before I chucked her and went after you instead." Kevin put on his biggest, most idiotic grin. "Ridiculous, huh?"

Amelia didn't look at him. She seemed to be staring out of the window. Kevin felt his heart sinking. He had the terrible thought that he'd blown it. By mentioning the possibility of romance he'd sunk their friendship. Amelia stood up. Her eyes had that faraway look. Kevin stood up too.

"Are you OK?"

Amelia seemed to snap out of it. She looked directly at him. She seemed nervous. Her voice took on a new, quiet quality.

"Helen was right, you know. I *was* jealous of you going out with her."

Kevin froze. It seemed like, in that moment,

their whole world had changed. Amelia was standing over two feet away from him, but he was sure that he could hear the loud thud of her heartbeat, that she could hear his.

"She was right about me, too," he whispered. "Most of it, anyway."

Kevin stared into Amelia's eyes. He could feel his chin trembling. It was a feeling he'd never had before. He wondered if it showed.

"So what are we going to do about it?" Amelia asked, softly, uncertainly.

Later, neither of them could be sure who made the first move. All they knew was how they were in each other's arms, kissing so hard that it almost hurt.

7

At first, it felt slightly strange, like she was playacting. But, by the second kiss, it felt like the most natural thing in the world. Kevin. Kevin was the one. He always had been. Without speaking, they sat down together on her bed, then kissed again, rolling over on the bed, pressing hard against each other, making up for lost time.

Amelia didn't want to be the first to speak. It might break the spell. She liked the way Kevin kissed – soft, yet urgent. She liked the way he didn't seem to take charge. Gently, he pulled away.

"I'm crazy about you," he said. "I always have been, really."

He smiled nervously.

"Me too." She smiled. "I've just been waiting till you were old enough."

Kevin put his arms round her again. "I grew up fast."

Soon they were on the floor, totally wrapped up in each other. That was why they failed to hear the front door open and close. Amelia's mum was on the landing outside when she called. "Amelia, are you home?"

She and Kevin broke apart as though their lives depended on not being caught. Amelia stood up and straightened her clothes.

"I'm in here, Mum."

The door opened. "Oh, Kevin, I didn't know you were here."

"Hi, Mrs Gorman."

If Mum noticed anything odd, it didn't show in her face. "I'm just making some coffee. Would you like some?"

Kevin looked at his watch. "Thanks, no. I lost track of time. I ought to get home for my dinner."

He got up and looked for his jacket, which Amelia knew had fallen down the side of the bed.

"Good day at work?" she asked Mum, to distract her.

"Is there such a thing?" Mum complained. "You just wait until you have to get a job, young lady. Then you'll realise how lucky you are now."

She closed the door behind her. Kevin had his jacket on.

"Do you think she noticed anything?"

Amelia shook her head. "I don't think we should tell – anyone – yet. Do you?"

"I don't," Kevin said. "This might take some getting used to."

"Yes," she said. "It might. I'll see you tomorrow then."

"Tomorrow."

They kissed again. Then he was gone.

Amelia looked at herself in the mirror. She still

had her school uniform on. Her hair was a mess. For once in her life, she looked her age. Impatiently, she pushed her hair back. Maybe I could put it in plaits, she thought. Then I'd look even more like a fifteen-year-old.

"Oh, Amelia," she asked aloud. "What are you getting yourself into?"

Dinner was steak pie, mashed potatoes and baked beans. Kevin wolfed it down in five minutes.

"You're in a hurry," his mum said. "Are you off seeing Helen tonight?"

"No. Not tonight."

Kevin hadn't thought about Helen since he'd left Amelia's house. His going out with her seemed a lifetime away.

"But she's still coming round for her dinner tomorrow, isn't she?"

"No. I don't think so."

He slurped down a glass of milk and stood up. "I'm going round to Pete's."

But he wasn't going to get away that easily.

"Hold on, Kevin. Have you two had a row?"

"Sort of."

"What happened?"

Kevin squirmed with embarrassment. It was bad enough telling your mum that your girlfriend had chucked you. But it was worse, trying to explain that you were really pleased about it. Luckily, Dad came to the rescue.

"Give the lad a break," he said. "He'll tell you when he's ready."

"That's right," said Kevin. "I will."

He hurried off before she could ask whether he had any homework.

Pete turned the sound down during the commercials. "Not seeing Scotty tonight?"

Pete had taken to calling Helen after the Star Trek character.

"Not tonight. Not any other night."

Pete seemed surprised. "You've seen the light, then."

"Something like that."

"Actually," Pete said, not looking at Kevin but at the TV screen, "I think Helen's all right . . ."

"Fine," said Kevin. "You go out with her then."

"That wasn't what I was trying to. . ." Pete started to say. But then the match started, and the conversation turned to the safer ground of England's team selection.

Kevin got home at ten.

"Helen called," his mum told him. "Twice. She sounded upset."

"It's too late to call her now," Kevin said. "I'll see her tomorrow."

"Wait a minute," Mum said, firmly. "I'm not sure that Helen will sleep easily unless you do call her. We women take romance very seriously, Kevin. You can't go round breaking young girls' hearts."

"It was her who chucked me!" Kevin protested.

"It sounds like she's changed her mind."

"Then that's tough," Kevin said, in a hard

voice. "She was getting too serious, anyway. She wanted to be with me all the time. She started acting hurt when I preferred being with my mates."

Mum smiled sympathetically. "Maybe you could discuss that, work it out?"

"I don't think so," Kevin said. "I think I'm better off out of it."

"That doesn't sound like you talking," Mum said, quietly.

Kevin grimaced. He knew that he was being cruel, but he could hardly explain about Amelia.

"You won't ring her then?"

Kevin shook his head. "I'm going to bed. I'll talk to her tomorrow."

But he knew that, if he could possibly avoid it, he wouldn't.

Amelia dawdled the next morning, spending extra time choosing which blouse to wear, then making herself up.

"You'll be late!" Her mum called up the stairs.

"It's all right. I'll catch the second bus."

"Then you'll definitely be late."

The second bus was an ordinary service bus, not a school one. It didn't stop right by the school, so you had to run like crazy to get to registration on time. Even then, it was often late. But Kevin always caught it, because doing his paper round didn't leave him enough time to catch the first one. And Amelia particularly wanted to see him this morning. She wanted to be sure that yesterday afternoon hadn't been a dream. The bus was just pulling up when Kevin came running down the street, shirt hanging out, bag trailing behind him.

"Hold on a mo'," Amelia asked the driver. Kevin jumped on.

"Thanks," he said.

This bus was a single-decker. They got a seat on the back row. The only other kids going to school were young ones. They were safe from observation. Kevin squeezed Amelia's hand.

"You can do better than that."

She leant round. They kissed – a long, drawn-out kiss. When it was over, Kevin smiled.

"Now I know that yesterday wasn't a dream."

"That was what I was thinking."

They kissed again.

"Can I see you to—"

He stopped. Amelia turned round. Dean Gates was getting on the bus. He, too, did a paper round. Amelia moved a couple of inches away from Kevin. He did the same in the opposite direction. By the time Dean looked round they were sitting farther apart than strangers might have done. Seeing Amelia, Dean walked the full length of the bus to join them. Ignoring Kevin, he pulled out his packet of cigarettes.

"Don't often see you on here," he said. "Want one?"

"No thanks. I've given up."

"Yeah? Saw you smoking by the mound yesterday. Saw you too, Atkinson. What did you do to make your girlfriend cry, huh?"

Amelia could feel Kevin bristle, but he said nothing. You didn't get into arguments with Dean Gates.

"You'll have to watch him," Dean told Amelia, blowing smoke all over her. "He's a real lady-killer."

The bus journey to school with Amelia left Kevin on a real high, despite Dean Gates' irritating presence. He was still floating on a cloud when he got to his second lesson, English. But seeing Helen's mournful face brought him down again.

"Hi," he said. "I would have phoned, but I didn't get in till late."

Helen ignored him. Good. That was the way he would prefer it. Except. Except he couldn't concentrate during the lesson, which was about a difficult poem called "Diary of an angry House-wife", or something like that. Except he kept remembering what his mum said yesterday evening – *that doesn't sound like you talking*. He didn't want to be nasty to Helen. So, when break came, he fell in step alongside her as they left the classroom.

"I thought you wanted to talk to me," he said.

"I changed my mind."

"Can't we be friends?"

Even as he said the words, Kevin realized that they were the worst cliché in the book. Helen snapped back. "You mean friends like you and Amelia Gorman? I don't think I could compete, could I?"

"Well, if you're going to be like that . . ."

Then Helen started crying again. They were in a corridor with lots of people around. It was embarrassing. He pulled a tissue from his pocket.

"Come on. Sit down."

He pushed open the door to the dining hall, which was empty but for one of the caretakers, rearranging tables. Helen cried some more. Then she wiped her eyes and tried to put on a brave face.

"I'm sorry," she said. "I shouldn't have said all that stuff yesterday. I just got jealous because I thought you preferred Amelia to me, though I know she only goes out with older boys and everything. . ."

She paused, out of breath. "But then I talked to Kirsty and to my mum and they both said that you were right not to want to get too serious and spend time with your friends and everything. So it was me, wasn't it? I blew it."

Kevin didn't know quite what to say.

"It wasn't just you," he muttered. "I didn't know how to handle things properly."

Helen gave him a weak smile. She was expecting him to say something else, Kevin saw. He wasn't going to ask her. But he couldn't stop her asking him. Her voice when she did speak was almost desperate.

"So, do you want to have another go? See if we can get it right this time?"

Kevin took a deep breath. "I . . . uh . . . I'm not . . ."

He swallowed and began again. "I'm sorry," he told her. "I don't."

Kevin thought that Helen would start crying again, but his rejection of her had the opposite effect. She stood up, eyes blazing.

"Then what are you being so *nice* for?" she

asked him. "Why didn't you just leave me alone? Damn you, Kevin Atkinson. Do you hear me? GO TO HELL!"

8

"What do you want to do tomorrow night?"

"I don't know," Amelia breathed softly. "Are your parents going out?"

"Don't think so."

"Neither are mine. Let's go to the pictures then."

"OK. You're on."

Amelia smiled, trying to think of something to say, but not in any hurry to fill the silence. In the background, she heard Kevin's mum shouting: "Kevin! Are you still on the phone?" His reply was muffled. He must have covered the receiver with his hand. Then, "I suppose I'd better go. Mum wants to ring somebody."

"OK," Amelia said. "I'll see you tomorrow. G'night."

"'Night."

Amelia put the phone down, feeling like she was in a fairy tale. Her initial uncertainties about going out with Kevin had all but vanished. He was so easy to talk to. Even the silences felt comfortable. It was a new, fresh world. She'd thought that she was in love with Rick, but that relationship seemed like a girlish fantasy compared to what she now had with Kevin. It was Friday night and Kevin couldn't see her because he had a football practice. But he'd rung as soon as he got in. Amelia was already missing him again. They'd only spent two evenings together so far — joking, kissing, cuddling, romping on the carpet in her bedroom like five-year-olds. Just two evenings, but it felt more like two years, they were so comfortable together. Amelia had never been happier. No one knew about them, yet. Soon they would have to tell their parents. Amelia didn't know how hers would react. It was one thing to be friendly with the cute young boy down the street, another to be rolling around the bedroom with him, night after night. And Kevin's mum and dad might think Amelia was corrupting their son, since she was over a year older than him.

Amelia went into the living room to join Mum and Dad watching "Cheers".

"Who was on the phone?" Mum asked casually, during the theme music.

"Just Kevin," Amelia replied. "I'm going to the pictures with him tomorrow."

"I was talking to his mum last week. She said he has a girlfriend now," Mum said, in the same casual tone.

"They split up."

Mum raised an eyebrow. "That was quick. Not on your account, I hope."

Amelia stared at the TV screen, trying to keep composed.

"No. *Of course not.* She finished with him."

Before Mum could question her further, the programme began.

Kevin came downstairs as Mum was finishing on the phone.

"Who was that you were talking to for so long? Helen?"

"No. Why would it be?"

Mum gave him an odd look. "It was just that when I picked the phone up, I heard you say something about going to the pictures tomorrow."

"That's right. I'm going with Amelia."

Mum didn't seem surprised. Kevin wondered how much more of the conversation she'd overheard.

"What are you going to see?"

"Depends what's on."

"You don't usually go to the cinema unless there's a film you particularly want to see."

Kevin was stumped for a reply. He wished he'd invented a film he was keen on. He could hardly tell Mum that he was taking Amelia out because she was still upset about splitting up with her boyfriend. He'd used that one too many times already. If anyone should be upset, it was him, over Helen. Instead he said, "Why are you going on at me? I just fancied seeing a film."

Mum shrugged. "I was wondering why you didn't arrange to go with Pete or Martyn."

"I'm going round to Pete's tomorrow afternoon and Martyn's coming here on Sunday. What's the big deal?"

Mum spoke calmly. "I think people might get

the wrong idea about you and Amelia, that's all."

Kevin stood awkwardly at the bottom of the stairs. He wished his dad was here. Dad always steered conversations away from uncomfortable subjects. He liked a quiet life. But Dad always spent Friday evenings with his mates in the pub and Kevin was cornered.

"What do you mean," Kevin said, "'the wrong idea'?"

"Well . . ." Mum said, with a trace of humour in her voice, "for somebody who split up with his first girlfriend on Monday, you've been remarkably cheerful this week."

Kevin didn't know what to say. Mum went on, "I know how much you like Amelia, Kevin. Sometimes, when you were younger, I thought you worshipped her a bit too much. You were really hurt when she moved schools and stopped seeing you all the time. But you slowly got friendly again. Now I get the feeling that you're beginning to see her in a different light."

Kevin spoke slowly. "You mean . . . like . . . my girlfriend."

"That's what I mean."

"What would be wrong with that?"

Mum sighed. "Nothing, necessarily. I know that the two of you get on really well. But she's a year older than you, Kevin. And girls grow up a lot quicker than boys. They have to. You're not experienced enough to satisfy a girl like her, love, no matter how mature you might be for your age."

Kevin was annoyed. "That's not the way Amelia sees it. She says my age doesn't bother her at all."

Mum was silent. Kevin realized that he'd given the game away. There was no point in trying to hide it now.

"We're serious about each other," he said.

Mum gave him a sad kind of smile. "I'm sure you are," she told Kevin. "But you're very young to be getting serious about any girl, particularly someone like Amelia. You don't need me to tell you that she's very . . . popular. She's had a lot of boys after her in the past and there'll be a lot more in future. I'm afraid that you'll get yourself hurt."

Kevin shook his head. "I can look after myself."

"Then I'm happy for you," Mum said. "I hope it all works out."

She didn't sound too optimistic.

The evening didn't start well. When Kevin and Amelia got to the front of the queue, the usher asked whether Kevin was fifteen, the lower age limit for the film.

"Of course I am," Kevin snapped, blushing, though his birthday was several weeks away.

"And so am I," Amelia added, putting on her sexiest smile, which did the job.

"We just have to check," the youth said, looking Amelia up and down.

Then there were three other Year-Eleven kids in the audience, so she and Kevin couldn't get too affectionate. The film wasn't much cop, either. They tried to leave as soon as the credits started, but Carla Hines, Jane Bullmore and Amanda Finch caught up with them. They were dressed up to the nines.

"Coming for a drink, Amelia? We're off to Gatsby's later."

"Not tonight, thanks."

The friendliness was a sham. These weren't girls who Amelia socialized with. They were winding her up.

"No, I suppose they might not let your boyfriend in," Carla teased.

Amelia knew that they didn't really think Kevin was her boyfriend, but she certainly wasn't going to give them the satisfaction of hearing her deny it. They got out of the cinema in a hurry.

On the bus, Kevin suggested that they go back to his house.

"Won't your mum think it's a bit late for me to be visiting?"

"I don't suppose so. She already knows I'm going out with you."

Amelia was taken aback. "You *told* her? I thought we agreed. . ."

Kevin interrupted. "She overheard us talking on the phone and guessed. I wasn't going to lie to her."

"Right. But . . ."

Amelia didn't know how to put it. She wasn't sure if she was ready for their relationship to come out into the open.

"I'm not sure if I can face them. I mean, I haven't even told my own parents yet."

"You're going to have to tell them. My mum's bound to talk to yours about it sooner or later."

"I guess you're right. What did your mum say when you told her?"

Kevin began to mumble, the way he did when he was embarrassed.

"She . . . she said I wasn't mature enough, that you might be using me as a stop-gap, until some older guy comes along . . ."

"What did you tell her?"

"That we were serious."

Amelia nodded. She thought that she *was* serious, but this evening had shown her that there could be problems ahead. She thought hurriedly.

"I'll tell you what," she said. "We'll tell them that we're going out on a kind of trial basis, until we're sure that it's right for us. That way, they'll see that we are being serious and mature about it."

Kevin nodded, but he looked hurt. "Who's on trial – you or me?"

"That's not what I meant at all," Amelia said, trying desperately to work out just what it was she *had* been trying to say. "All I meant was a way to keep our parents happy."

"OK," Kevin said. "We can call it a trial. As long as you're sure that we're not keeping it quiet because you're embarrassed to be seen with me."

Amelia was embarrassed, because that was exactly what she had been thinking. She needed time to get used to having a younger boyfriend, or at least to prepare the ground with her friends.

"We don't have to hide it," she told him. "You can tell anyone you want."

The moment these words were out, she regretted them. But then they were kissing, and most of the doubts vanished.

*   *   *

"I've brought Amelia back for a coffee."

Kevin's dad stood up. "It's good to see you, Amelia. Film any good?"

"It was OK. I've seen better."

"Hello, Amelia." Kevin's mum was more reserved.

"Hi, Mrs Atkinson."

She took a deep breath. If she was going to make a speech, she had to do it quickly, before she lost her nerve. "I think Kevin's told you about us."

Mrs Atkinson gave her a smile, but it was a frosty one.

"In a way."

"The thing is ..." Amelia stuttered out, "we know that it might be awkward – me being older and all – but we really care for each other, so we want to give it a try. We're going to take it slowly at first, so that, if it doesn't work out, we can stay friends. I hope. . .I hope that's OK with both of you."

"Of course it is, Amelia," Mr Atkinson said. "We're very happy for both of you. Aren't we, dear?"

Mrs Atkinson smiled, more warmly this time. "Yes, we are," she said. "Thank you for explaining, Amelia. I appreciate that."

Upstairs, in Kevin's bedroom, Amelia was uncomfortable.

"It's no use," she said. "Now I've spoken to your mum and dad, I have to speak to mine. I want to get it over with tonight. Do you mind?"

Kevin walked her home. There was still a light on in her parents' living room.

"How do you think they'll take it?" Kevin asked.

"Probably accuse me of corrupting a minor, the way your mum nearly did."

Kevin laughed. They kissed for a long time. A light came on in the hallway.

"I'll call you tomorrow," she told Kevin. "G'night."

"Amelia?" her mother's voice called.

She put her key in the door and opened it.

"I'm glad you're still up, Mum. There's something I want to tell you."

9

On Sunday afternoon the lads came round to Kevin's place to watch the Italian football. At half time, Kevin threw into the conversation that he and Amelia were 'sort of' going out.

"What do you mean 'sort of'?" Pete wanted to know.

"Dunno. I mean, she's my girlfriend."

"Wants a toy boy, does she?" Martyn said, trying to be funny but sounding awkward. Kevin didn't reply.

Then Pete came out with: "Are you. . .you know?" And he gave Kevin a sort of funny wink. Kevin didn't reply, but he could see what they were both thinking. If Kevin was going out with a girl as sexy as Amelia Gorman, it wouldn't be long before he scored. Yet, over the last week, sex had been the last thing on Kevin's mind. After all, it was only a month since he'd first kissed a girl. Things were going fast enough for Kevin as they were. He'd only just got into the first division. He wasn't ready to play in the Premier League. But maybe Amelia was. Maybe she already had done. He hoped she hadn't.

But that night it had preyed on his mind. Suppose Amelia expected him to ... what was the word? *Perform*. She'd also expect him to be responsible. A month ago, Kevin had thought of losing his virginity as something in the dim and distant future, like taking his driving test. But now here he was on Monday, standing in front of the pharmacy counter of Boots, inspecting at least twenty different varieties of condom. How did you choose between "Safe", "Extra-safe", "Sensitive", "Super strong" and "Ribbed for extra stimulation"?

Finally, he settled on the one with the plainest packet. There was no point in getting flustered about it. He was hardly likely to use them, after all. The woman behind the counter didn't even look at Kevin as he paid. He walked out of the shop quickly, expecting to bump into Amelia's dad, or one of his teachers – someone who would instantly know what he'd been buying. But he met no one.

"You're late, Kevin. Did one of the teachers keep you in?"

"No", Kevin told his mum. "Course not. I just went into town for a computer magazine."

"No need to bite my head off, young man. Had a bad day?"

"'S alright."

Kevin went upstairs to get changed. He was on edge, but it had nothing to do with school. This would be the first time he'd been round to

82

Amelia's house since she'd told her parents about them. Now he understood how awkward she'd felt on Saturday. Here he was, after years of being her "friend", turning into her "boyfriend". It was almost like he'd lived the previous fourteen years under false pretences.

After school on Monday, Amelia went back to Gilli's with Karen. She'd neglected her friends for the last week. Amelia had to tell them about Kevin before they found out some other way. But at first it was hard to get a word in edgeways. Gilli had had a date on Saturday – her first since the summer – and wanted to give Amelia a blow by blow account of it.

"And he kept going on and on about how his dad worked for the Rank Organization, so he gets free tickets to lots of things. Like I was meant to be falling over myself to go out with him again. I have never met anyone more *boring*. . ."

"You're getting boring now," Karen interrupted. "I had the full half-hour account yesterday. What did *you* do on Saturday, Amelia?"

Amelia cleared her throat.

"I went to the pictures with my new boyfriend."

That got both girls' attention immediately.

"Who?" Karen asked. "No. Let me guess. Mike Slater?"

Amelia shook her head.

"My turn," Gilli said. "That friend of Rick's who always fancied you – David Joyce?"

Amelia shook her head again.

"You've not started up with Rick again after all

that moaning about 'we have nothing in common'?" Karen asked.

"No," said Amelia. "I don't think you'll get it." She left a dramatic pause. "I'm going out with Kevin."

"Little Kevin?" Gilli asked, incredulously.

"He's not that little any more."

"You told us he was going out with a girl in the Fourth Year!" Karen said.

"Well, he's not any more. He's going out with me."

"Blimey," Gilli said. "Amelia's got a toy boy."

Karen smiled. "I think it's really good," she told them both. "Kevin's really nice. Congratulations."

"Yes," said Gilli, 'it's good. I can see the headlines in *Westtown Weekly* already – *Amelia Dares to be Different*. Now tell us all about it."

Amelia gave her friends a rundown of the last four weeks, from her feelings of jealousy when Kevin first started dating Helen to their first kiss after school just a week before.

"And what's happened since?" Gilli asked, with a mischievous tone to her voice.

"Nothing, if you mean what I think you mean," Amelia said quickly.

"So how did your mum and dad take it?" Karen wanted to know.

"Actually, they were dead nice about it. Mum said how she'd always thought it was a pity Kevin was a year younger than me not a year older, as we're so perfectly matched. And Dad started talking like Kevin was about to become his son-in-law!"

"Sounds like relief to me," Gilli sneered.

"What do you mean?" Karen said.

Gilli gave one of her famous, condescending smiles.

"Look at it their way. One minute Amelia's dating a hunk in leathers with a motorbike, so they're worried about you getting killed, or pregnant or just running off with him. The next minute she's dating someone barely out of short trousers whose idea of debauchery is a feel under her sweater."

Amelia laughed. "Maybe you're right. Maybe they are relieved. But they're wrong to be. Kevin's growing up fast."

"You mean you're teaching him!" Karen teased. "You know what you are, Amelia Gorman, corrupting the youth of Coddington – you're a cradle snatcher!"

"You're just jealous because you fancy him yourself," Gilli told her, sharply.

"I prefer them a bit younger myself," Karen replied. "There are plenty of nice looking boys in the Second and Third Year. I go off them when they get acne and start to shave."

All three girls laughed. Then Karen changed her tone.

"Seriously though, Amelia, you know that some people at school will really get at you over this, don't you?"

"That's their problem."

"Maybe. But you and Kevin will feel the heat."

"We're up to it," Amelia told the two girls, "as long as our friends stick by us. I think we're in love."

Gilli and Karen looked at each other. Then, almost in unison, they said: "This girl seems serious."

"Where'd you go after school?" Amelia asked Kevin. "You caught a different bus."

"I went into town," he replied, slightly secretively. "I wanted to pick up a computer magazine."

Amelia wondered why he hadn't got the magazine from the newsagent who he worked for, but, before she could ask, there was a familiar knock on the door. Mum. Mum never normally came up when she had someone in her room.

"I thought you two might like some coffee."

Mum brought in the tray. Kevin thanked her politely and chatted with her for a couple of minutes about school. But Amelia was seething with anger. Now that Kevin was her boyfriend, Mum was changing the rules. She wasn't giving them as much privacy.

"What's wrong?" Kevin asked when Mum had gone.

"I've got this nasty feeling that Mum isn't going to leave us alone," Amelia said. "We'll never know when she's going to turn up checking that we haven't got all our clothes off."

Kevin laughed. "Well," he said, "she's just been, so I'd say we're pretty safe for half an hour. Unless she decides to come back for the dirty mugs, that is."

Amelia grinned. Kevin got on the bed and kissed her, as passionately as any boy had kissed her before. Even so, Amelia felt a little strange.

"You seem a bit tense," Kevin said, gently.

"Sorry," Amelia said. "I'm still mad at my mum."

"Don't worry," he said. "She's not coming back. She knows what we're doing."

Kevin kissed Amelia again. Despite what he'd just said to her, the atmosphere in the room had changed. Amelia's mum's invasion of the room made both of them a bit awkward. Kevin forgot about the packet in his pocket – they weren't going to go any further than they'd gone before. Maybe they wouldn't have done anyway. He didn't mind. Actually, it was sort of a relief. After a while, he broke off and drank some tepid coffee.

"What do you want to do on your birthday?" he asked her.

"I don't know yet," Amelia said. "I haven't really thought about it."

Kevin pressed her. "It's less than three weeks away."

"You're right," Amelia reflected. "A few months back, Mum and Dad did say they might let me have a party. But I've had a lot on my mind recently. What do you think?"

Kevin nodded. "Sounds OK."

Actually, he'd been thinking of a quiet night somewhere special, just the two of them. A party was way too public.

"You don't look too sure," Amelia said.

"No, it'd be good," Kevin said. "I'd get to know some of your friends . . ."

"You could bring some of your friends, too." Amelia told him. "I'd like to get to know those lads you're always seeing – Martyn and Pat."

"Pete," Kevin corrected. "Yeah. I'm sure they'd like to come."

"Good. I'll talk to mum and dad about it," Amelia said. "We'll need to get a move on."

She put her arm round Kevin and cuddled him, the way she used to now and then before they were going out. Kevin tried to smile convincingly. Inside though, he thought that the party was a bad idea. He would be on display in front of all of her friends. He wasn't sure if he was ready for that yet. And if Martyn and Pete came along, the age difference would be even more blindingly obvious. Maybe Amelia's mum and dad would talk her out of it, Kevin thought, with a glimmer of hope. But he knew that he was conning himself. One thing about Amelia: she always got her way.

10

Paul Sykes was in the same Maths group as Amelia: intermediate level. He was tall and athletic looking, with ginger hair. He often contrived to sit with Amelia and Karen.

"Hi girls."

Karen smiled and Amelia nodded.

"There's a party on my house Saturday. Want to come?"

Amelia thought for a moment. If she went to Paul's party, she'd have to invite him to hers and her parents had said no more than thirty kids . . . Before she could reply, though, Karen did.

"Love to. Is it your birthday?"

"Nah, but my folks are away for the weekend. They said I could have a few mates round." He paused. "Will you two be . . .uh. . . coming on your own?"

He was looking at Amelia but it was Karen, again, who replied.

"I will." She turned to Amelia. "But I don't . . ."

"I'll see if Kevin can come," Amelia said, quickly. "I'll let you know."

Paul looked curious. "Kevin?" he said. "Have I met him?"

"Probably," Amelia told him. "Why don't you just wait and see?"

Before Paul could dig any deeper, Mr Flawn came over and asked when they planned to do any work.

"Paul Sykes!" Kevin said. "His lot are all into heavy metal and seeing how much ale they can down before throwing up."

"No, they're not," Amelia told him, laughing. "Paul's nice."

"Everyone's nice to you," Kevin said.

"You mean boys."

"Yes," Kevin said, assertively. "Boys, because they want to go out with you."

"You make it sound like I encourage them all!" Amelia protested.

"I know you don't, but even so, when people are on their best behaviour you don't get to find out what they're really like. I'm not sure about Paul. I know his younger brother."

"Steve?"

Amelia was dimly aware that Paul had a younger brother, but he was in the year below Kevin. It hadn't occurred to her that Kevin had friends who were younger than him.

"That's right, Steve. Paul's always beating him up."

Amelia shrugged. "Isn't that something all older brothers do to younger brothers?"

"Maybe," Kevin said. "I wouldn't know."

Amelia felt foolish. Kevin, like her, would

have liked a younger brother or sister. Her parents had chosen not to have more children. His weren't able to, and somehow that made it worse.

"You'll come, anyway," she said. "Won't you?"

"I'll think about it," Kevin said, reluctantly. "Does he know I'm going out with you?"

"Not yet."

"Didn't you once tell me he had a crush on you?"

"That was ages ago," Amelia said.

Actually, it was only last term, but she wasn't going to tell Kevin that. Amelia couldn't help it when boys got crushes on her. It was flattering in some ways, irritating in others. Sometimes, Amelia felt sorry for them and found it hard to let them know she wasn't interested.

"Gotta go," Kevin said. "See you later."

Lunchtime was about to end. Amelia picked up her bag. She was about to go to the form room when Jane Bullmore came into the social area.

"Hey, Amelia!"

Amelia stopped. Even from a few feet away, Jane smelt of smoke. Amelia hadn't had a single cigarette since she first got together with Kevin.

"There's this rumour going round," Jane said.

"Rumour?"

Amelia knew what was coming.

"That lad you were just talking to – the one we saw you with on Saturday. What's his name? Atkinson."

"Kevin? What about him?"

Jane gave a sort of awkward look out of the side

of her eyes, as if she was apologizing for what she was about to say.

"People are saying that you're going out with him."

Now Jane was joined by her cronies, Carla and Amanda. Amelia could see that they were expecting her to deny it. Whatever she told these three, it would be all over the school by afternoon break. But there was no backing out.

"Yes," she said, firmly. "I am going out with him."

Carla and Amanda burst into a fit of giggles. Amelia decided that she hated them, that she would never speak to them again. But Jane kept a straight face.

"I don't get it," she said, in a serious voice. "You have lads eighteen, twenty after you. You could have anyone. And instead you go for a kid who hasn't started puberty yet. This is a wind-up, isn't it?"

Amelia shook her head. "He's the one I want," she told them. "You'd better get used to it."

Amelia got up to go. Jane turned to Carla and Amanda.

"It looks like we've got a child molester in our year," she said.

"Is that the best you can come up with?" Amelia said, bitterly. "You're sick."

She walked out of the room. Behind her, the three girls chanted, "*Cradle snatcher! Cradle snatcher!*"

Amelia cringed. When Gilli and Karen teased her with that phrase before, it was faintly amusing. But now it was embarrassing, even a little threatening. And it was only just beginning.

"Is it true?"

Chris Monk joined Kevin under the shower. Chris had just beaten his friend at badminton. It had been a long game and they were the last into the changing rooms.

"Is what true?"

"That you're going out with Amelia Gorman."

"Who told you?" Kevin asked, irritated. "Martyn or Pete?"

Water spun from Chris's hair as he shook his head.

"Neither of them. I heard a bunch of Fifth Years talking about it, afternoon break. So, how long have you been going out with her then?"

"Since last week."

"And how far have you got?"

Kevin frowned and punched Chris on the shoulder.

"None of your . . ."

"Hey!"

Kevin had meant to punch Chris playfully, but he'd hit him too hard. His friend slipped against the tiled floor, lurching, naked, against the wall. There was a loud crack as he banged his head, then fell to the floor. Chris moaned. Kevin swore loudly.

"Are you all right?"

Chris tried to get up, holding his head. Kevin had to help him.

"I'm sorry, Chris. It was a complete accident. I'll take you to the nurse."

Chris shook his head. He was clearly dazed.

Kevin helped him out of the showers. There were still a couple of boys getting changed.

"Get Mr Trout!" he called out to them. "Chris has banged his head." Then he sat the boy down. Chris began to dry himself, automatically. Kevin started trying to apologize again, but no words came out. By the time the teacher arrived, Chris was getting dressed.

"What happened?" Mr Trout asked Kevin.

Before Kevin could answer, Chris said, "I slipped in the shower, Sir. I banged my head but I'm all right now."

"We'll just see about that, shall we?"

Mr Trout felt Chris's head and tested whether he had concussion.

"You'll live. But be more careful in future. Were you messing around?"

"No, Sir."

"People don't generally fall over without a reason."

When the teacher had gone, Kevin thanked Chris for not telling on him.

"I didn't mean to hurt you," he said. "It's just that, when people talk about Amelia, I get a bit sensitive."

"Not as sensitive as my head is now," Chris muttered. "Go home. You'll miss your bus."

Kevin checked his watch and saw that Chris was right. Awkwardly, he patted him on the shoulder, said "sorry" again, and hurried to where the buses left. He started to feel guilty as he ran. Perhaps he should have offered to walk home with Chris, who lived locally. But that would have been even more awkward. He would have to find some way to get back into Chris's good books.

Kevin was aware of some peculiar looks as he got onto the bus, but nobody on the lower deck said anything. He was just in time. As he climbed the twisting staircase, the bus set off to Coddington. He hoped that Amelia had managed to save him a place on the top deck. As Kevin climbed to the top of the stairway, the jeering began.

"Here he is!" A taunting voice called out, "Amelia Gorman's toy boy!"

There were more ugly voices – all of them belonging to girls in the Fourth and Fifth Year – as Kevin found his way to the vacant seat next to Amelia. He didn't look back, and she didn't look around. Kevin put down his bags and then put his arm around Amelia's shoulder. Immediately there was a loud "oooooooooh" from the back of the bus, followed by rude comments from a couple of the lads.

"This been going on long?" he asked her.

"They've been teasing me since I got on the bus," Amelia told him. "They were calling me a child molester earlier."

This made Kevin seethe, but he tried to keep calm.

"They'll get fed up of it quickly," Kevin told Amelia, trying to conceal his anger. "They're just jealous."

"I hope you're right," she muttered. "I couldn't take this every day."

After a couple of minutes, most of the cat-calling stopped. Amelia tried to hold a conversation with Kevin, but he found it hard to join in. His head was burning up. He wanted to hit someone. Chris Monk was an accident, but some of these people were asking for it.

"Have you decided about the party on Saturday?" she asked.

Kevin mumbled. "Will any of these bozos from the back be there?"

"I don't think so. Maybe. We'll face them out."

"I dunno," Kevin said.

He wanted to refuse to go, but couldn't come out with it.

"Look," he went on. "I won't know anyone there, apart from you. Maybe we should wait until your party, where we're more on home ground."

"You don't understand," Amelia told him, urgently. "I want all this to be over by the time we get to my party. I don't want to have a party where I'm worrying about whether people will insult my boyfriend or call me a *cradle snatcher* behind my back. Come on Saturday. It's just a party. We don't have to stay that long. . ."

"OK," said Kevin. "If you really think that . . . oof!"

A heavy bag had clouted Kevin in the side, knocking all of the wind out of him. There were loud laughs from behind.

"Watch out, toy boy!"

Kevin turned to see who had assaulted him. The burly figure of Dean Gates was disappearing down the stairway. Kevin started to get up. Amelia grabbed him.

"Don't be a fool. You can't fight Dean. He'd murder you!"

"I can't let him get away with that!"

"You haven't got any choice."

The bus stopped and Dean got off. The couple sat in silence. Three stops later, they left the bus too, a shower of sniggering jibes following them down the stairs.

"I can't believe it!" Kevin said, once they were alone on the path. "How can people be so immature?"

"You said it," Amelia told him, gently. "Jealousy." She paused. "Maybe we should sit on the lower deck for the time being."

"What?" said Kevin, "and let them win? No way."

He put his arm round her waist. His side was still hurting, but he wasn't going to let Amelia know this. She was the most important thing in the world to him and he wasn't going to let Dean Gates or anyone else get between them.

"You were right," he told her. "I have to come to that party. We have to face them out, show them that we're together and we don't care what anybody thinks about it."

Amelia turned to him, and smiled. Letting his bags drop to the ground, Kevin put his other arm around Amelia. Somehow, when he held her like this, nothing else seemed to matter. They kissed passionately and the pain in his side began to retreat. They stood there for what seemed ages, locked in an embrace. Then a passing car honked its horn. Kevin and Amelia waved at it, then carried on kissing. Kevin held Amelia still closer, feeling like the luckiest boy in Coddington. He didn't care what anyone said. It was him and her against the world now. No one was going to get in their way.

11

Amelia slept badly that night, worried about the onslaught of teasing to come. But, as it turned out, Kevin was right. After a couple of days, the novelty seemed to wear off. Wednesday wasn't too bad. Thursday was worse, because Kevin had a football practice after school, so people kept asking where he was. By Friday, they were old news. Only Dean Gates, who had clouted Kevin with his bag on Monday, kept giving them hostile stares. But Dean was like that, slow in every way.

"Do you want to come round tonight?" she asked Kevin as he walked her home.

"I told Pete I'd go round to try out this new game he's bought."

"Oh. OK. I'll see you tomorrow night then."

"How are we getting there?"

"My dad said he'd give us a lift."

"Fine."

"You're all right about this party, aren't you?" Amelia asked him.

"Yeah. Sure."

Amelia had never known how to deal with Kevin when he went monosyllabic on her. She was going to ask him in for coffee, but sensed that he wanted to get away, so left it. They kissed again. Kevin grinned and took off. As he walked home, he seemed to take on a swagger, as though, the further from Amelia he got, the lighter his step became.

Amelia rang Gilli. "Aren't you seeing Kevin tonight?"

"No. He's playing *computer games*."

"Gross. Still, if you will go out with a fourteen-year-old . . ."

"I know," Amelia sighed. "Want to come round?"

"Go on then," Gilli said. "I'll get the bus after dinner. You asking Karen round too?"

Amelia paused. She really wanted to talk about things with Gilli one to one, on an equal footing. Gilli had had several boyfriends, but Karen had yet to go out with anybody, and her self-pity about this sometimes spoiled conversations.

"No," Amelia said finally. "Not tonight."

"Oh," said Gilli. "OK."

However, the consequence of not inviting Karen was that they spent the first part of the evening talking about her.

"We've got to get her a boyfriend," Gilli insisted. "There must be someone who's going to be at this party that she likes."

"I thought that Karen liked anybody in long trousers?"

Gilli laughed. "So that rules out all of Kevin's friends, doesn't it?"

"Ouch," said Amelia. "I suppose I asked for that."

"Though that lad, Pete – he's nice looking."

"That's where Kevin is tonight. I'll make sure he asks him to my party."

"Good," said Gilli. "But we still need to set her up with someone for tomorrow night. What about Paul himself?"

Amelia shook her head. "He's over a foot taller than her for a start. And I don't think he really notices Karen. He talks to her in Maths, but it's me he's looking at all the time."

"At least he talks to her though," Gilli said. "Not many boys do."

"Not many boys know how to talk, full stop," Amelia replied.

"But Kevin does," Gilli said, smiling.

"Yes."

"You ought to hang onto him then."

The game finished and Kevin ejected the disc.

"So where you going with Amelia tomorrow?" Pete wanted to know.

"A party. Paul Sykes."

"Rather you than me."

"You don't have to tell me."

"Paul isn't so bad, but some of his mates . . ."

Kevin didn't need it rubbing in. "Maybe I'll persuade Amelia to leave early."

Pete raised an eyebrow. "I thought she had better friends than that."

Kevin shrugged. "I dunno. You don't really choose your friends, do you?"

Pete looked at him quizzically. "Speak for yourself."

Kevin grinned. "What are you doing tomorrow then?"

"Pictures."

"Persuade Martyn to go, did you?"

Pete glanced at the ceiling. "Nah. Someone else."

Kevin didn't catch on for a moment. He was about to load another game when he worked it out.

"You mean a girl?"

Pete smiled condescendingly. "You're not the only one with hormones, you know."

"Who?"

Pete shook his head. "Not telling."

"Come on, I told you about Amelia."

"Only because I'd have found out for myself."

Frustrated, Kevin tried to think of a way to wheedle the story out of Pete. But Pete was a man of few words. Maybe his girlfriend could get him to talk. Kevin couldn't.

"You'll bring her to Amelia's party, though, a fortnight tomorrow."

"If I'm still going out with her then, maybe."

Pete began to sort through his games. "This one?"

He held up a box. Kevin ignored it. "So she's not from our school, this girl?"

"I'm not saying. I don't really know her yet."

Kevin's curiosity intensified. "Is tomorrow a first date, then?"

"Sort of."

Before Kevin could ask another question, Pete loaded the game, signalling that the conversation was over. A minute later, they were immersed in

'Death Dealers from Davros', and all thoughts of girls were banished from their minds.

Amelia had bought a large plastic bottle of cider.

"Are you sure I shouldn't have brought something too?" Kevin asked, as they stood in the hall, waiting for Amelia's dad.

Kevin hardly drank, and Amelia didn't want the added embarrassment of a boyfriend bringing soft drinks to a party.

"A big bottle between two is plenty," she told him.

Amelia wore black jeans and a low-cut, sequinned silk top, with a silver cross hanging between her breasts. Kevin wore the pink shirt and bright tie he'd had on at the wedding in August. He didn't look right. Amelia tried to work out how to tell him.

"I don't think anyone will be wearing ties tonight," she said, casually.

"No?"

He whipped it off and undid the top button of his shirt.

"Better?"

Amelia frowned. A look of concern spread across Kevin's face. Amelia thought of offering him one of her baggy T-shirts. But he might be offended. And someone at the party was bound to recognize anything of hers he wore. Kevin would be teased about it, which would make matters worse.

"Do the top button up," she said.

Kevin did as he was told.

"That looks better, more stylish."

He smiled nervously. Amelia put her arms round him.

"You look great," she said.

"So do you."

As their bodies pressed against each other, Amelia felt a warm pulse of desire. They kissed. The kiss felt so good that Amelia was tempted to suggest that they stayed at home instead. Gilli could look after Karen. Who cared what people said about her and Kevin? He was right before. It would be better if her friends met him properly at her birthday party, where there would only be people who Amelia had invited. But, as she was thinking this, her father came into the hall, car keys in his hand.

"Ready?"

Kevin nodded, and put his coat on. It was too late. Amelia put on her leather jacket. Kevin took her hand. They went and sat together in the back seat of her father's car.

Paul Sykes lived on the edge of the new town. As they drove through the town centre, Amelia spotted Karen, waiting at a bus stop.

"Dad, can you pull over?"

Karen hadn't seen them. Amelia had to get out of the car and shout to her. A bus was pulling in and, for a moment, Amelia thought that Karen hadn't heard her. But then her friend came running over.

"Great, thanks," she said, getting into the back seat of the car even though the front passenger seat was free. "It's a long walk from the bus stop to Paul's house. I wasn't looking forward to it."

"You're right to be wary," Kevin said. "There are some strange people out – tonight especially."

"Why tonight?" Karen asked.

"Because they're all going to Paul Sykes's party!"

Everyone laughed.

"You look great," Kevin told Karen.

That was Kevin, always ready to give someone positive strokes. And, actually, Karen did look good. It was warm in the car and she had taken her coat off. Karen had on a short, tight black skirt over black velvet leggings, and a loose chiffon blouse. She had on long silver earrings, too, and plenty of make-up. She looked five years older than she was.

"Yes, Karen, you look brilliant," Amelia told her, wondering whether her friend was overdressed, worrying whether Kevin fancied Karen tonight more than he fancied her.

"So do you," Karen said, then she spoke to Kevin. "It's nice to get to meet you properly. I mean, I see you around at school but you don't exactly talk there, do you? And you're never round at Amelia's when I'm there."

"I thought that Kevin had been practically living in our house since he was old enough to walk over," Amelia's dad said, from the driver's seat, much to Amelia's embarrassment.

"It's so romantic," Karen said. "Childhood sweethearts."

Amelia could feel Kevin blushing.

"We were never sweethearts," Amelia said. "More like brother and sister, until twelve days ago."

"Unless you were kidding yourselves," Karen replied, mischievously.

Amelia was uncomfortable having this conversation with both Kevin and her father present. She was relieved when Dad pulled up outside Paul's house.

"If you want to come back before half eleven," Dad said, "you can give me a call. Otherwise, I'll be outside the house then. Don't keep me waiting. OK?"

Amelia nodded and said goodbye. Karen was already almost at the doorway of Paul's house. It was a cold night and Amelia shivered, zipping up her jacket for the short walk to the house. Already, there was loud music booming from the front room. Across the street, a baby cried. Coloured lights shone through the curtains. The bulbs had been changed for red downstairs, green up. Surely the wrong way round, Amelia thought. Karen was knocking on the door. On the pathway, Kevin put his arm around Amelia, his body surprisingly soft, and warm.

"There's something I want to tell you before we go in," he said.

"What?"

"In case it goes badly and you hate me before the evening's over."

"Don't be daft," Amelia said. "What is it?"

Kevin spoke softly. "Karen and your dad were right. I have been in love with you since I was old enough to walk. I always will be, too. As long as I can walk, you won't be able to keep me away from you."

He held her close to him. Amelia whispered in

his ear. "That's the most beautiful thing that anybody's ever said to me."

She wanted to tell him that she loved him too, but, at that moment, Karen called from the open doorway.

"Come on, love birds, it's time to party!"

They went inside.

12

The first people Kevin spotted at the party were two girls from his year at school: Louise Tuttle and Nicky Fish. Nicky was in his form. Kevin nodded hello to them. Both girls ignored him. Kevin followed Amelia upstairs, where they put their coats in a back bedroom. On the stairs going down, they met their host, Paul Sykes. Paul said hello to Amelia. He looked silly, Kevin thought, in his bleached Mudhoney T-shirt and jeans that had been deliberately ripped at the knee. Then Paul noticed Kevin.

"Who invited you?" he said, angrily.

Kevin felt his face flush. Before he could say anything, Amelia broke in. "Kevin's with me, Paul. We're going out with each other."

Paul's face dropped. He looked from Kevin to Amelia and back again, his expression going from incomprehension to incredulity.

"Er, all right," he said, finally, and continued up the stairs.

"Not everyone knows about us, then," Kevin said to Amelia.

"So it would seem."

Avoiding the booming music in the front room, they went into the kitchen to get a drink. Kevin was relieved to see that not all of the people at the party were from his school. Amelia introduced him to Andy Carrogan, who went to the Sixth Form College, and his girlfriend, Tracey. Andy, a tall, athletic type, was a friend of Amelia's ex, Rick. He and Amelia began talking about a concert they'd both been to earlier in the year. Kevin made polite conversation with Tracey.

"Are you at the Sixth-Form College, too?"

"No, I'm at St Theresa's. I've got another year before college."

St Theresa's was an all-girls Catholic Comprehensive.

"How do you know Paul?"

"I live on the estate," she said. "We play sports together sometimes. Mind you, when he asked me, I didn't know it was going to be quite like this."

She pointed to the living room, where bodies were beginning to crash against the walls, out into the hall, and back in again.

"I think they call it slam dancing," Kevin said.

"I thought that went out of fashion years ago," Tracey said. "I prefer slow dancing, myself."

As she said this, Tim Coyne, a Fifth Year from Westtown, came out of the living room wrapped around Kerry Barton. Kerry was one of the best-looking girls from Kevin's year. They had always been friendly.

"Hi, 'melia," Tim burped.

Amelia hated her name being shortened, but

smiled politely. Kevin nodded at Kerry. She ignored him, instead turning to Tim and whispering in his ear. Tim gave Kevin a funny look, grabbed a can of beer, then left. As Kevin watched them push their way into the room where the dancing was, the front door opened. Gilli came in, with a group of people who lived near her. One was a lad from the Fifth Year, Mike, who Kevin got on with. Soon, introductions were being made and Kevin was having another drink. The evening was going better than he'd expected.

Amelia felt relieved. There had been no jibes, no teasing, only the occasional nasty look. And not everyone here was from Westtown Comp, either. Andy Carrogan was the only one of Rick's friends she'd liked: a good looking, kind bloke who actually listened to what you said to him and didn't just talk about himself. She was enjoying herself. Kevin seemed to be having a good time, too. He was talking to Mike Slater, a thin, good looking boy from her year, about football. Then Gilli said: "Strange that Karen hasn't arrived yet."

Amelia realized that she hadn't seen her friend in the half hour since they arrived.

"No, she's here," Amelia told Gilli. "We saw her in town and gave her a lift."

"Then where is she? We're meant to be finding her a bloke, remember?"

Amelia nodded. She turned to Kevin. "We're just going to see what's happened to Karen."

"OK."

Gilli glanced out of the window and shook her head. It was too cold for anyone to be outside.

"You don't think she's upstairs, do you?" Amelia asked Gilli.

"I doubt it. She'd have had to work pretty fast, wouldn't she? And the toilet queue is moving, so she can't be in there."

"What about this room?"

Between the kitchen and the living room was the dining room, which had a small notice saying "Not in Use – Keep Out!" taped above the door knob.

"Worth a try," Gilli said.

Amelia tried the handle. It wasn't locked.

"Karen?"

The room was dark and appeared to be empty. But, when Amelia opened the door a bit further, she could make out a couple on the floor beneath the curtains at the other end of the room.

"Karen?" Gilli whispered.

"It's not her," Amelia said.

They closed the door. "In that case," Gilli said, "she must be in. . ."

Another body banged against the door of the living room, knocking it open. Amelia recognized the music coming from the room at an almost unbearable volume: it was a group Rick used to like. The door closed again.

"Do we have to go in?" Amelia said.

Gilli nodded. "Let's do it together."

They opened the door. Amelia made an instant decision not to invite any of the people inside to *her* party. The furniture was shaking. Through the red haze, beyond the frantically dancing schoolboys, Amelia could see beer stains on the walls. She could also see Karen. Her small friend

111

was drenched in sweat. This was probably a result of the way she was jumping up and down. She was leaping higher and higher, in time with Paul Sykes. She saw Gilli and Amelia and grinned.

"You're missing all the fun! Come on!"

"A bit loud for us," Gilli called, but it didn't look like Karen could hear her.

Neil Wynne, from Amelia's English group, pushed his way up to her.

"Amelia, you look fantastic! Let's have a dance."

Amelia shook her head politely. "Not my kind of music."

"I'll get Paul to change it."

"No, really. It's OK."

The door opened. Andy Carrogan stuck his head round it.

"It's getting a bit too crowded out here," he told Amelia. "We're going to another party. Join us if you like."

"No thanks."

Amelia would have liked to have left immediately, but she wasn't sure that the invitation included Kevin. Andy looked sorry.

"See you then."

Neil, ignored by Amelia, pushed his way past Andy out into the hall. Andy's girlfriend, Tracey, tried to wave goodbye to Paul, but he didn't notice, too absorbed in Karen. Gilli looked at Amelia and shrugged.

"To each their own."

They tried to get out of the room, but the hallway was crowded. Paul had said he was only going to invite a few people, but things had clearly got out of hand. Someone had pulled the sign off the dining room door and it was full of people. Gilli joined Mike Slater, and was soon engrossed in conversation with him. Amelia looked around for Kevin, but couldn't see him. She looked in the kitchen. It was so hot in there now that someone had opened the back door. But Kevin wasn't out there either. Mike and Gilli were leaning against the dining room wall, talking. Amelia didn't like to interrupt them. However, a couple of minutes later, when Kevin still hadn't appeared, she did.

"Mike, did you see what happened to Kevin?"

Mike shrugged. "Some lads from school arrived and started talking to him. They might have gone outside."

"Outside? What on earth for?"

"To cool down, maybe. It was hot in there. That's why we moved in here."

Amelia returned to the kitchen. Nearly all the drink, she saw, had gone. The new arrivals, mostly boys from her year, still had their coats on. They were clutching the bottles they had brought with them. There was no sign of Kevin. Amelia saw a pretty girl from his year standing by the kitchen door, which was now closed again.

"Excuse me – Kerry, is it? – have you seen my boyfriend, Kevin?"

Kerry Barton turned away from the older boy who was chatting her up. She looked at Amelia with disdain, then jerked her head towards the door.

"I think he's having a *private conversation* outside."

Hurriedly, Amelia opened the door. The first thing she saw was two girls, both Fourth Years, giggling as they looked out into the garden. Then Amelia saw what they were looking at: three boys from her year, Keith Manners, James Patton and Mark Fisher. They had someone on the ground. And they were kicking him.

"Maybe now you'll learn. . ."

"Keep your hands off our girls . . ."

"Don't look so pretty now, do ya?"

"Leave him alone!" Amelia shouted.

She began to run towards the boys, who ignored her. That was when the girls grabbed her from behind.

"You stay out of this."

"Let go of me!"

Amelia pulled herself clear of the girls. "What's wrong with you? It's all right for you to chase after older boys but you can't stand it if I go out with a younger one?"

"That's exactly right," said the more surly of the two girls.

The other girl let loose with a stream of obscenities. They blocked Amelia's path to Kevin, who was still on the ground, being kicked. Amelia had to think quickly. There were too many of them. She ran back into the house, pushing her way through the kitchen, looking for a friendly face. She couldn't find Gilli and Mike. She shoved her way through the crowded hall and into the living room. There was no longer room to dance. The throng inside the room was more like a football crowd. In a corner, Amelia could see Paul and Karen, kissing. She called out his name. He couldn't hear her. No one could hear anything over the noise.

Amelia pushed her way to the hi-fi. She couldn't see which switch to touch, so she took the easier option. Reaching down behind the stereo console, she pulled the plug from the wall. Instantly, the music stopped. Before any of the throng had a chance to complain, Amelia bellowed at Paul.

"There's a bunch of your mates beating up my boyfriend outside. You've got to go and stop them NOW!"

Paul hesitated for a moment, but then Karen started to push her way over to Amelia.

"Come on!" she called to the boy she'd just been kissing.

He followed her, as did several of the others. In the hallway, Mike and Gilli joined them. Amelia could hear Paul talking to himself as he came after her.

"Where did all these people come from? No one's supposed to be in there!"

Then they got outside. Kevin was on the ground, curled up in the foetal position. Keith, James and Mark were still standing over him, laughing. Seeing the posse arrive, the two younger girls quickly got out of their way.

"Get off him!" Paul shouted. "Who invited you anyway?"

For a moment, Amelia thought that there was going to be a bigger fight. But when the bullies looked round they saw that they were outnumbered. Amelia walked straight through them and lifted Kevin to his feet. He smiled weakly.

"I was beginning to wonder when the cavalry would arrive."

She helped him walk back, slowly, into the house.

13

The party ended. Once Paul realised how many gatecrashers had got in, he had no choice but to break it up. While this was going on, Kevin was in the bathroom with Amelia. He cleaned himself up the best he could, but his nose kept bleeding. He knew that he'd have trouble riding his bicycle on his paper round in the morning. His pink shirt was torn. It was also covered in black marks from the boots that had kicked him. He'd have to throw it away. In the hallway, Karen kissed Paul goodnight. She had been helping him to clear up, but there would still be a lot of explaining to do when his parents got back the next day. Amelia came downstairs with their coats. She helped Kevin on with his then put her arm around him. Even this hurt.

"Are you sure you don't want to go to casualty?" Mr Gorman asked, in the car.

"I'm sure," said Kevin, deeply embarrassed that Amelia's dad was seeing him this way.

"At least we can take you back to our place, find you a clean shirt."

"Really," said Kevin, "I just want to get home to bed. Nothing's broken. I'll survive."

They drove back in silence. When Kevin got home, much to his relief, Mum and Dad were still out. He had a quick shower. Then, still wet, without even drying his hair, which he looked after so carefully, he lay down on his bed and fell instantly asleep.

When Kevin's alarm went off, seven hours later, it seemed that every part of his body was in pain. Slowly, Kevin got up. He wasn't sure that going out with any girl was worth pain like this. Nevertheless, he made his way downstairs, shovelled some crunchy nut cornflakes down his throat and got his bike out of the shed. It took him two attempts to get onto it.

Since he started going out with Amelia, Kevin had worked out a kind of ritual with his paper round. He had changed the order so that he always did her house last. It made the whole round a kind of quest to get to Amelia. The Gorman family were late risers, so they hadn't noticed that their *Independent* arrived fifteen minutes later in the week and a half hour later on Sundays.

Today, however, the round took twice as long as usual – two hours, instead of one. It was gone nine when Kevin got to the Gorman house, and Amelia's dad was up. In fact, he was in the driveway, washing the car. He gave Kevin a friendly wave.

"Had to do something to fill in time," he told Kevin, pointing at the car, "with no paper to read."

"I'm sorry about that," Kevin said. "I'm a bit slow today."

"I'm surprised you turned in at all," said Mr Gorman. "You must be aching all over. Couldn't someone cover for you?"

"They could," Kevin said. "But then I wouldn't get paid, and I'm saving up."

Mr Gorman smiled and took the paper. "No need to tell me what for."

He paused. It was an awkward silence. Kevin was perched on his Raleigh bike, one foot held in by a toe-clip, the other on the ground. He was about to go when Mr Gorman spoke again. "I expect you feel pretty small about what happened last night. I know that would have been my first reaction."

Kevin nodded.

"But if a bunch of bruisers decide to beat you up, there's not much you can do about it."

"I guess not."

"Amelia's very upset. She thinks she shouldn't have left you on your own."

"That's ridiculous," Kevin protested. "She couldn't stop a bunch of idiots finding me if they want to."

Mr Gorman nodded. "That's what I told her, but she'll need to hear it from you. I expect she'll come round to see you later. Got many more papers to do?"

Kevin shook his head. The conversation – the longest one he'd had with Mr Gorman – was over. He cycled home, intending to go straight back to bed. But it wasn't to be. Mum caught him at the bottom of the stairs

"You're back late today."

"Uh huh."

She moved closer to him. "What happened to your nose? It looks like it's been bleeding."

"It's nothing."

"And what about this?" Mum said, holding up his ruined pink shirt from the night before. "This which I found stuffed in your bin. Is this 'nothing' too?"

Amelia got up late, having slept badly. When she got downstairs at eleven she was surprised to find that Mum was still reading the paper. She said so.

"It arrived late," Mum told her. "Kevin was on the slow side this morning."

"He did his round?" Amelia asked, incredulous. "After last night?"

"He's a very proud boy."

"I know."

Amelia poured herself orange juice. She sat down and looked for the fashion page which they usually had on a Sunday.

"I suppose it was a bit embarrassing for you last night," Mum said.

"More than a bit," Amelia said, cringing as she remembered it all. "First Paul threw out the yobbos who beat up Kevin, then he threw out everybody else . . . so it looked like it was Kevin's fault the party ended early."

"He hadn't been drinking, had he?"

"Kevin?" Amelia shook her head. "You'd have to force feed him to drink more than a glass of cider."

"So it wasn't his fault at all?"

"Course not. They just arrived at the party, heard that he was there with me and dragged him outside."

Mum shook her head. "I do wish sometimes we'd got you into a better school. All those rough children from the new town. . .and you're not getting anywhere with your exams."

"That's not to do with the school," Amelia said. "I'd hate it even more if you'd sent me away to some posh, private school. I'm just not academic, that's all."

Amelia didn't want to have the monthly career conversation her mother inflicted on her, so she finished her juice and got up.

"I think I'll go and see Kevin, find out how he is."

"Good idea," Mum said. "But tell me one thing, Amelia."

"What?"

"You're not going to drop him, are you, because of all this trouble?"

Amelia answered uncomfortably. "No. Of course not. Why would I?"

"You said you were giving the relationship a trial. I wondered if the trial was over."

"We've only been together a fortnight," Amelia complained. "So it's going to take a bit longer for people to get used to us being together. That's their problem, not ours."

"I hope you're right," Mum told her.

Amelia knocked on the Atkinsons' back door with trepidation. She wouldn't be surprised if Kevin's mum blamed her for the beating last night. But Mrs Atkinson welcomed Amelia warmly.

"Let me make you some coffee. You can take one to Kevin."

"Where is he?" Amelia asked.

"He's up in his bedroom," Mrs Atkinson said, "nursing his wounds."

"I'm so sorry about last night," Amelia said. "I keep thinking that it must have been my fault somehow."

"That's silly talk," Kevin's mum told her. "But I hope none of those boys are coming to your party."

"Only Paul," she told her. "The one who broke up the fight. He's going out with one of my best friends."

Amelia took the coffee upstairs to Kevin's room. She had both hands full, so didn't knock, but announced, "it's me", as she pushed the door open.

"Huh?"

The curtain was drawn. Kevin was in bed, asleep.

"Hi."

Kevin blinked, and started to sit up. He looked incredibly vulnerable and sweet.

"Stay where you are," Amelia said, putting the coffee down. "I'll join you."

She pushed the bolt across on Kevin's door, then took her sweater off and squeezed into the bed beside him. A smile spread across Kevin's face. They hugged, then kissed. Kevin groaned. Amelia kissed him harder. Kevin groaned again.

"The spirit is willing," he told her, "but . . . look, could you get out of bed, please? You're hurting me!"

When she'd stopped feeling like a fool, Amelia examined his bruises.

"You look dreadful!" she told him.

"You should see the other guys," Kevin quipped. "I might have bruises, but they're *ugly*!"

Amelia laughed. They drank their coffee in a comfortable silence. Eventually, Amelia worked out that Kevin was waiting for her to leave before he got up. He had homework to do, he told her.

"So do I," she said. "That's why I'm here."

Soon though, she left. Kevin was seeing his friends that afternoon, the way he did every Sunday. Amelia tried to phone Gilli but she was out. Then she caught Karen, but she was just about to go over to Paul's.

"The house is still a mess, but his parents don't get back till this evening. We should be able to straighten it out. At least, that's my excuse for going round."

"You'd better watch out," Amelia told her. "He'll have you ironing his shirts next."

Karen laughed. "I'll do whatever I have to do to hang onto him."

Amelia paused. "But do you *really* like him, Karen? I mean, for himself, not just because you happened to get off with him last night."

"What do you mean," Karen said, "'happened to get off'? Paul's been trying to work up the courage to ask me out for weeks, he told me. He only had the party because he thought that I'd come."

"Really?" Amelia said. "That's great."

She remembered how she'd thought that Paul was still after her. She'd believed that Karen was included in the party invitation only out of politeness. Before Amelia could get the conversation started up again, Karen announced that she had to get going. They agreed to make a trip to the Body Shop together after school the next day. Amelia hung up, then, reluctantly, did some homework.

It was hard to concentrate. Amelia kept thinking of Kevin, covered in bruises. She loved him so much, but he was so young, so vulnerable. She worried about the party. There were only thirteen months between them but, on that night, he would be fourteen and she would be sixteen. For four weeks, the gap between them would be even more immense. Would they be able to bridge it?

14

"I suppose it was too much to ask," Gilli said, as they walked across the High Street towards the Body Shop, "all three of us having boyfriends at the same time."

Gilli looked forlorn. She'd spent most of Saturday night talking to Mike Slater, but he hadn't asked her out, or even tried anything on.

"He's so nice," Gilli protested. "It's not as though he's shy."

"He is nice," Amelia agreed. "And you get on well with him. That doesn't automatically mean you have to go out with each other."

"Sounds like a good reason to me," Karen said.

"Maybe he's gay," Amelia suggested. "A lot of people are."

Gilli hadn't considered this possibility.

"You'll find someone else," Amelia reassured her. "No problem."

"We're not all like you," Karen said. "We don't all have boys falling over themselves to ask us out."

It was a shame, Amelia thought. They were supposed to be celebrating Karen's first boyfriend. Instead, they were concentrating on cheering Gilli up. Still, there were only twelve days to go before her party. Hopefully, Amelia could fix Gilli up with someone there.

Karen held up a tub of peppermint foot lotion.

"Tell me, Amelia, does Kevin like to suck your toes?"

"Not after Saturday night."

As they tried out different blushers, Amelia described her boyfriend's bruises.

"Hasn't it made you think twice about going out with Kevin," Gilli asked, "if it's going to cause all that aggro?"

"Are you saying that I should dump him because he got beaten up for me?" Amelia replied, aggrieved.

"That's not what I said," Gilli replied. "All I meant was that the hassle isn't going to go away."

"Of course it will," said Amelia. "Eventually, people will get used to the idea of me and Kevin together."

"Eventually," said Gilli, "sure. Eventually, you'll both be in your twenties and no one will care if one of you's thirteen months older or younger than the other. But while you're both still at Westtown Comp, it mightn't be so easy."

"You're exaggerating," Amelia told Gilli. "It won't be that bad."

"For both your sakes," Gilli said, "I hope you're right."

*   *   *

It was funny how preparation for a party occupied so much of the next twelve days. It seemed to Amelia that Paul Sykes's was an example of everything a party shouldn't be. Hers would be the opposite.

Funny too, how people started to be nicer to her, knowing that there was a party in the offing. Oh, there were still the occasional whispers of 'Cradle snatcher' and stuff like that, but these came mainly from Fourth-year girls, and Amelia couldn't care less what they thought of her. The boys who had beaten Kevin up stayed well out of her way. If Kevin was getting any problems from them, he didn't mention it to her. Her other mission for the party was to set Gilli up with someone.

"How about Andy, who was at Paul's party?" Karen suggested. "He was nice."

"He had a girlfriend," Amelia remembered. "Tracey – a really pretty girl."

"She's a friend of Paul's," Karen told her. "I don't think they're serious."

"I'll tell you what," Amelia said. "I'll give Andy a ring, invite him to the party, and tell him to bring one of his mates, if he likes. That way, even if he's with Tracey, we get another spare bloke for Gilli."

This plan was agreed. Amelia's only worry was that there would be too many boys at the party. She had a maximum number of thirty guests, and she already had sixteen boys invited. Two of them were Kevin's friends, though. They didn't really count, she decided.

Kevin wasn't sure whether he was looking

forward to the party or not. He hadn't seen that much of Amelia over the fortnight between Paul's party and hers. He'd been saving up for a present, so couldn't afford to go out much. Also, he had his first GCSE coursework assignments due in, and didn't want to mess them up. Kevin thought of himself as OK at school – not especially clever and not very quick with work. But he usually kept up with his more academic friends, like Pete, by working harder than they did.

Since Paul's party, it had become clear to Kevin that every girl in the Fourth Year had a down on him. Why that should be wasn't clear. Kevin didn't want to discuss it with Amelia. She seemed to think that they were getting over all the age difference problems. Kevin didn't want to remind her of them. He was careful to stay out of the way of Fifth-Year boys. That was easy enough. But he couldn't avoid the girls he shared classes with.

At the beginning of term, Kevin got on well with the girls in his year. In some lessons, he was often the only boy in a small group. This suited him fine. He preferred working with girls, in many ways. He preferred their company. They were more mature, and helpful. They had more laughs – not the boys' silly games, like hiding people's pencil cases or flicking paper around, but entertaining gossip about music, TV and people in the school, stuff like that.

Since they'd heard that he was going out with Amelia, however, there were no girls who would let him work in a group with them. Kevin was forced to work on his own in some lessons, or with boys whose behaviour annoyed him. And the girls, from a distance, seemed worse behaved, too. They were sillier, some of them, and laughed hysterically at ridiculous things – the smallest sexual innuendo, the way somebody spoke. . .

It was only a minority, Kevin supposed, who had it in for him. Helen Scott, in English, no longer worked with him, but she wasn't nasty. This was ironic, he thought, since she was the only girl who had a right to hate him. Life would be so much easier, he sometimes thought, if he was going out with Helen, instead of Amelia. He wouldn't have to put up with Fifth-Year boys sneering "toy boy", whenever he walked by them. He wouldn't have to watch his back every time he went to the toilet.

Kevin had bought Amelia a silver, heart-shaped pendant on a chain. The pendant was a corny gift, but sometimes corny ideas were the best ones. On the back of the pendant, he'd had engraved "from K to A" with a large "X". Amelia could keep a tiny photo of him in it, if she wanted. He had one of her in his wallet, a holiday snap from Greece last year, which he'd begged from the Gorman family album. It would be nice, he thought, to have a picture with the two of them together. He'd borrow his mum's compact camera and take it tonight. Pete was coming to the party, with his mysterious girl-friend. Martyn said he'd come, too, but Kevin suspected that he might bottle out. Amelia had offered to invite other boys from his year. The only other one Kevin could think of was Chris Monk. They hadn't had a game of badminton since Kevin accidentally knocked Chris over. These days, when they played football together, Chris rarely passed him the ball. Kevin tried to engineer a conversation with Chris a couple of times, but Chris avoided him. So Kevin didn't invite him.

Mum had bought Kevin a new black shirt to replace the pink one destroyed at Paul's party. He buttoned it up to the top, and wore black jeans with it, then checked his image in the mirror. The black set off his blue eyes and blonde hair. Tonight was his night. So what if most of the people at the party were going to be older than him? He was going out with the best looking girl in the school. And it was her party. Tonight, Kevin was on equal terms with everyone else. The party a fortnight ago was history.

"You look very smart," his mother said. "It's raining out. I'd better drive you."

And she did, even though it was only a five-minute walk. Kevin gripped the tiny package in the palm of his hand.

"I'm sure she'll like it," his mother told him, before he hurtled through the rain to her front door.

Amelia looked ravishing. She wore a new grey silk top with huge black dots on it, and black denim jeans.

"You look terrific," he told her, when they'd kissed.

"So do you."

Kevin gave Amelia her present. She seemed delighted with it, and put it on straight away. Unfortunately, the chain was quite long, and you couldn't see the pendant beneath her blouse.

"You're not meant to, silly," she told him. "It's a kind of secret, that's the whole point of it."

Amelia made him promise to bring her a picture small enough to fit in it the next day.

"I want to take a picture of us now," he told her.

He got his mum's camera out of his coat and, between them, they worked out how to set the self-timer button. They put the camera on its side on the table at the bottom of the stairs. Then they stood in the hallway with the door behind them, waiting for the first guests to arrive. The machine began to whirr.

Amelia turned to Kevin. "You realize that anything I might want to do with you later is now illegal."

Kevin smiled. "All the best things are."

"I love you," she told him, making his heart leap, "even if, tonight, you *are* two years younger than me."

"I love you too," he replied. "Happy birthday."

As their lips came together in a kiss, the flash went off. Moments later, they were interrupted by the doorbell ringing for the first time. Amelia let in Gilli, Karen and Paul.

"We're not too early?"

"No, no," Amelia said, "come in. I'll put some music on."

"Don't let Paul choose it," Gilli warned.

Kevin took their coats. Paul came with him. He was dressed more smartly than at his own party, Kevin noticed – no rips in his jeans, a clean Consolidated T-shirt.

"I'm really sorry about what happened the other week," Paul said. "No hard feelings?"

He offered Kevin his hand. Kevin shook it.

"No hard feelings."

The next person to arrive was Martyn.

"I'm not staying long," he told Kevin. "Just thought I'd make an appearance."

Kevin tried to introduce his friend to Amelia, but she was upstairs showing Gilli the portable compact disc player her parents had bought for her birthday. When she came downstairs, the deluge of guests had started arriving – mostly Fifth-Year boys and girls who Kevin knew only vaguely. Amelia kept introducing them and Kevin forgot their names almost as quickly. Martyn looked out of place, as he was the only person there wearing a sweater. He stuck close to Kevin's side.

"Ah," he said, sounding relieved. "Here's Pete."

Kevin looked round to see his friend giving him a half wave with his free arm. The other arm was around his girlfriend, who Kevin had been waiting to meet. Pete's partner turned out to be an attractive blonde girl in a long, old fashioned dress which Kevin recognized. He recognized the girl wearing the dress, too. It was Helen Scott.

15

The party, Amelia quickly decided, was a flop. Despite the anarchy and early finish of Paul Sykes's party a fortnight before, people had talked about it for days afterwards. Hers, she was certain, would be forgotten by tomorrow. Nearly everyone had arrived now (everyone she'd invited, in fact, except for Andy Carrogan, who she hadn't spoken to, only left a message for). But nothing much was happening. Amelia had carefully selected good dance music, most of it recent chart stuff, but only a handful of people had danced during the last hour and a half.

There were two or three couples smooching. These included Karen and Paul, still in the first flush of romance. Gilli looked a bit fed up. Kevin and his friends were keeping to themselves. What was more, one of them had brought, and seemed to be going out with, Helen Scott. Amelia's friends chatted to her and said they were having a good time. Behind her back, Amelia was sure they were discussing the fact that Kevin's ex-girlfriend was here. But there was nothing she could do about that. She wanted to introduce Kevin to her friends, on equal terms. But Kevin was being surprisingly uncommunicative tonight.

Amelia finished a dull conversation about a Michael Jackson concert she'd seen on video. Then she marched over to where Kevin and his friends were standing. As she arrived, the fat one, Martyn said: "I'm off now, Amelia. Thanks for the party."

Amelia started to say "don't go yet", but she could see that it would make no difference. Soon, other people would start to leave, even though it was only just gone eleven. The party had no spark, no spirit.

"We need to liven things up," she said to Kevin and Pete. "Let's start some dancing."

"If *we* start it up," Helen said pointedly, "I don't think your friends will join in."

"Who cares?" Kevin said, before Amelia could respond. "Let's have some fun. C'mon."

Kevin took Helen's hand and Amelia guided Pete to where the dancing was supposed to be. Kevin turned the sound up. Simply Red boomed from the speakers. It was a slow song and Pete held Amelia uncomfortably, like he thought the eyes of the party were on him. They probably were. Helen had been right. No one joined them, not even Paul and Karen. Paul, Karen had told Amelia earlier, could only do the sort of dancing that involved throwing yourself around the room. Amelia looked across at Kevin. He was holding Helen closely, not paying attention to anyone else. They looked natural together. Amelia felt pangs of jealousy. To any of her friends watching,

Amelia was the weird one here, inviting fourteen-year-olds to her sixteenth birthday party. What was she trying to prove, and to whom?

Maybe it was the volume of the music which made her miss the door bell. Or perhaps Martyn let her final guests in on his way out. The first thing that Amelia knew about it was as the song was finishing and a familiar tall figure stood in the doorway.

"Amelia! Happy birthday!"

Andy Carrogan was holding a small bunch of pink carnations.

"These are for you. Thanks for inviting me."

He kissed her on the cheek.

"You did say it was all right for me to bring a friend."

"Yes, of course. Is Tracey. . ."

"Nah, we split up. But I think you know this guy. . ."

Amelia looked over Andy's shoulder. She saw a handsome, well-built man in a leather jacket, holding a birthday card. He gave her a wry smile. For a moment, she was too nonplussed to smile back. It was Rick. Once she'd got over the surprise, Amelia was pleased that Rick had come. After all, Kevin's ex-girlfriend was there. This evened the score. And the two Sixth-formers certainly livened up the party. Rick produced some cassettes from his pocket.

"I remembered your taste in music. Thought you might need these. Guaranteed to bring the house down."

Amelia winced, but let him change the music. The party needed a jump start. As he went up to the hi-fi, Rick nodded at Kevin and Helen. Amelia watched as Kevin nodded back. She realized that, annoyingly, Rick would assume that Kevin was there with Helen. He had seen them together at the pictures, after all. She would have to make the real situation clear. But that might be awkward.

The familiar opening bars of "Smells Like Teen Spirit" thundered from the hi-fi. Suddenly, it seemed that everyone at the party was on the dance floor. Amelia was separated from Kevin. She found herself dancing opposite Andy. Beside her, Karen and Paul began hurling themselves around. For a moment, she worried about the furniture. Then she reminded herself that she wasn't middle-aged yet. This was her birthday. She was supposed to be having fun.

From then on, the party took off. Time seemed to rush by. The party was raucous, but not wild. Amelia spent most of her time dancing. She was pleased with her choice of guests. There were no attempts to sneak into the bedrooms upstairs, no drink on the carpet, no one being sick in the bathroom or smoking dubious substances. Yet everyone was having a terrific time. Except, maybe, Kevin. Amelia danced with him a couple of times, but, as hostess, she had to dance with a lot of people. She danced most with Andy Carrogan, because he asked her most and because he was a good dancer. She had one dance with Rick. He managed to get her during a slow song.

"I should never have let you go," he told her.

"As I recall, it was the other way round."

"Yeah, but if I hadn't been so proud. If I'd called

you, told you how I really felt, I could have got you to change your mind . . . couldn't I?"

Amelia looked into his deep brown eyes. He meant it.

"I don't know," she said. "Maybe."

"But it's too late now?"

She looked at him again. Rick leant closer towards Amelia and kissed her softly on the lips, taking her by surprise. It was the first time she could remember that he'd kissed her so gently and for a moment she was thrown. How could she be in love with Kevin yet still be tempted by Rick?

"I'm afraid it is too late," she whispered, keeping her voice friendly.

Rick shook his head. "I had my chance. I blew it."

The next thing Amelia knew, Kevin was beside them. Amelia saw anger shooting across his face. She looked around. Across the room, Gilli saw the panic in her eyes and began to walk over. Amelia wasn't sure what to do. She didn't want to explain the kiss with Rick in front of both boys. So she acted as though it hadn't happened and he couldn't have seen it.

"Where's Helen and Pete?"

"They just went home."

"Oh."

Rick looked confused. "Your girlfriend left with another guy? That sounds like bad luck."

Kevin's face reddened. "She's not my . . . ."

A new, loud song began. Amelia interrupted, shouting over the music, "Kevin's going out with me now."

Rick looked even more confused. Before he

could say anything else, Gilli was by Amelia's side. She whispered something to Kevin and he walked off, into the hall.

"Do you remember Gilli?" Amelia shouted at Rick. "I think you met . . ."

Rick smiled. Gilli smiled back. She was looking good, Amelia thought, making the most of her size. With her hair let out, and a low-cut, backless dress, she could pass for a younger version of Kathleen Turner.

"You want to dance?" Rick asked her.

"I'd love to."

Amelia followed Kevin out into the hall.

"It was just a kiss," she hissed at him. "A friendly peck. No big deal."

"Did I say anything?" Kevin hissed back.

"No. But your face did."

"I was just surprised to see your ex-boyfriend here, that's all."

Amelia raised her voice. "No more surprised than I was to see your ex-girlfriend!"

"That's different. She was with someone."

"Well I didn't know that . . ."

"Children, children . . ."

They both looked around. Karen stood next to them, smiling condescendingly. "I realize that this is your first row, but don't you think you'd be better off having it in private?"

Amelia nodded. Kevin looked embarrassed.

"Come on," said Karen. "It's a great party. Why don't you come and have a dance with me, Kevin? Everyone's having a good time."

"Well, I'm not!" Kevin snapped back.

And, with that, he went to the cloakroom,

grabbed his jacket, and stomped out of the front
door, into the rain. Amelia stared at the door in
a daze.

"Aren't you going after him?" Karen asked.

Amelia shook her head. "That's the first argument I've had with him since he was ten, but I
know what he's like when he gets pig-headed
about something. He has to go off for a while until
he cools down."

"You think he'll be back?" Karen asked,
doubtfully.

"Yes," said Amelia.

But she knew Kevin, and she knew that he
wouldn't be back tonight. In an odd sort of way,
she was relieved.

Two hours later, most of the guests had gone.
It was down to the hard core now. Amelia's
parents had come home from the friends that
they were having dinner with, checked for
damage, and gone to bed. They hadn't com-
mented on Kevin's absence, probably hadn't
noticed it. Amelia saw Karen and Paul to the
door, where they had a taxi waiting. That left
Andy, Gilli and Rick. Andy stood in the hall,
looking slightly ill at ease.

"I'm ready to go," he said. "But I'm not sure
about . . ."

He pointed to the back room, where Rick and
Gilli were spread across the sofa, locked in a passionate embrace.

"It seems a shame to interrupt them," Amelia
said, "but . . . do you need to call a taxi?"

Andy shook his head. "I've got my mum's car.

I'll be all right," he added hurriedly. "I've not had much to drink."

"I noticed," said Amelia. "Very responsible."

She smiled at him. Andy looked nervous, which wasn't like him. "Look," he said. "I'm not very good at this."

"At what?" Amelia replied, gently.

"At asking people out."

"Oh."

Half of Amelia was excited and half of her dreaded having to turn Andy down. He was too nice.

"Rick told me the score about you and Kevin," Andy went on. "How you've been friends since you were kids and you've been seeing him since you split up with Rick."

"That's right," Amelia said.

She was glad that she didn't have to explain.

"But you aren't that serious with him, are you? I mean, I noticed he left earlier."

"Past his bedtime," Amelia joked, then felt guilty for sounding so callous. Somehow she felt embarrassed, explaining to Andy that she and Kevin *were* serious.

"It's hard to explain," she said. "We've known each other for a long time."

Andy nodded. "All I want to know is, if I was to ring you up, in, say, a couple of weeks, and. . . uh. . .ask you out. . .would I have a chance?"

Amelia hesitated. "I don't know," she said, slowly. "If I wasn't going out with Kevin, I guess you would. But . . ."

Her voice trailed off. Andy gave her a broad smile. "I'm glad that's over. Do you think that I could give you a birthday kiss now?"

Amelia knew that this was getting dangerous. She could feel the closeness of Andy's body to her. He was warm and handsome and it was her birthday and she was a little drunk and she hadn't been kissed properly since the party began.

"Yes," she murmured. "Every chance."

Five minutes later Rick and Gilli walked into the hall. "Sorry to interrupt," Gilli said, "but we're ready if you are, Andy."

Reluctantly, Andy broke away from her. He pulled his car keys from his pocket and gave Amelia a debonair smile. "I'll call you," he said.

Gilli gave Amelia a funny look, then put her arm around Rick. "Great party," she said.

"Thanks."

Then they were gone. Amelia climbed the stairs to her bedroom. She kicked off her shoes and looked at herself in the mirror. She didn't look a day older, but she felt like she'd aged a decade. Without getting undressed, she lay down on her bed and pulled the cord which switched off the light. Then she started to cry. How could she have betrayed Kevin that way? He was the love of her life. She was sure of that. Wasn't she? Suppose he found out about her kissing Andy? He'd chuck her straight away. Amelia couldn't bear that to happen. She loved him. She'd told him so tonight. Yet Kevin had behaved so childishly earlier. He wasn't ready to go out with someone like Amelia yet. Tonight had made that very clear. And she had always carried a bit of a torch for Andy Carrogan. He was by far the nicest of Rick's friends. Andy was mature, kind and very good looking. She hadn't invited him for herself, she had invited him for Gilli. But now that Andy had made it very clear he wanted her, Amelia couldn't help being tempted.

Why was life so confusing? One minute, everything seemed so simple, the next it was all falling apart. Amelia wished that Kevin were here now, to hold her, to make love to her, to make everything all right. But he wasn't and it wasn't. Tired and frustrated, Amelia sobbed herself to sleep.

16

Kevin had made a fool of himself. He knew
that. He needed to make amends as quickly as
possible. That morning, he was the first to
arrive for the papers and did his round in record
time. He intended to go straight back to bed,
as he usually did on a Sunday. But when he
got back, he was too hyped up to sleep. He
needed to go and see Amelia, to apologize.
But there was no way that he could go round
there before noon. He went down to the kitchen
and went through the drawer where Mum put
all the old packets of photographs. The most
recent ones were from a holiday they'd had in
Guernsey, back in June. Kevin took the packet
up to his room and went through the pictures
carefully. He needed to select one that was the
right size, but which also showed him looking
his best. After a while he found it. The picture
showed him on a beach, posing with the sea
behind him. He wasn't smiling, exactly, but
he was tanned and his eyes had that cheeky
expression which people seemed to find attract-

ive. It would do, Kevin decided. That was, if Amelia still wanted to wear him next to her heart.

Kevin had over-reacted. There was nothing wrong with an ex-boyfriend giving Amelia a peck on the lips. He might have done the same to Helen, if it had been her birthday. But it was the look on her face. It was the hours of boredom beforehand. He'd had to pretend to enjoy himself while her friends ignored him. It was everything.

He'd walked round for what seemed hours the night before. At first, he was trying to calm down. Later, he was trying to work up the courage to go back to the party. Twice, Kevin had walked past Amelia's house. The first time, he hadn't had the bottle to go back in. The second time, Amelia's parents' car was in the drive, and he'd assumed that the party would be finishing. That was when he'd given up and gone home to bed, where he had found it hard to sleep. Eventually, at half past eleven, he couldn't stand it any more. He walked over to her house.

"She's still in bed," Mrs Gorman told Kevin. "She had a very late night, but then, you know that, don't you?"

Kevin nodded. Clearly, Amelia's mum didn't know that he'd left early. Equally clearly, she wasn't going to let him go up to her room.

"I'll tell her you called by. I expect she'll come and see you."

"OK."

Kevin left. He was meant to be round at Pete's

that afternoon, but he didn't go. He didn't want to talk about Amelia and he didn't want to talk about Helen, either. "I expect she'll come and see you," Mrs Gorman had said. It wasn't much of a promise, but it was all he had. He could hardly go round to the house again without showing himself up. So he would stay at home, hoping she'd call.

"Not watching the football this afternoon?" Mum wanted to know.

"Got too much homework to do."

In truth, Kevin had cleared his homework so that he would have a completely free weekend. But he went upstairs anyway, so that his mum wouldn't start questioning him about Amelia's party again. He should have gone round to Pete's. Amelia would assume that he was out. He was always busy on Sunday afternoons, which irritated her. Maybe she'd gone out, too. Who with?

By leaving the way he did, Kevin might have thrown Amelia back into the arms of Rick Jones. Suppose she had got off with Rick, as a way of getting back at Kevin? Suppose she was out with him now, on the back of his bike somewhere, in the cool October sun? Kevin couldn't stand it any more. He went downstairs and picked up the phone.

"I'm sorry, Kevin, she's out," Mrs Gorman said.

"Do you know where she is?" Kevin tried to keep his voice natural.

"She caught the bus over to see her friend Gilli about an hour ago. I'll tell her you called."

Kevin put down the phone. At least she was with Gilli, not with Rick. Kevin went back to his room and lay down. She would call him when she got home. He was very tired. He could use an hour's sleep. He curled up on his bed and tried to calm himself down. Everything would be all right. She would call him when she got home. Everything would be all right. She would call. But it was no use. Sleep wouldn't come. He lay on the edge of the bed, waiting for the phone to ring. He had dozed off when it did ring, two hours later. Somehow, Kevin managed to wake himself up, hurtle downstairs and pick up the phone before Mum or Dad could get to it.

"Hello?"

"Kevin? How are you?"

Kevin sighed. "I'm fine, Gran."

He made polite conversation with his grandmother, who always rang on Sundays. They only talked for five minutes, but it felt more like an hour. Kevin spent every moment worrying that Amelia was trying to get through. But, as it turned out, she wasn't.

"I don't know how you could have finished with him. He's so gorgeous."

Amelia shrugged. Gilli was ecstatic that she was going out with Rick.

"He has his faults," Amelia told her friend, "as I'm sure you'll discover."

"Nobody's perfect," Gilli replied. "Talking of which, have you spoken to Kevin yet?"

Amelia shook her head. "He always sees his mates on Sunday afternoons."

"The kids who were at the party?"

"Those are the ones."

Gilli gave Amelia a long, hard look. "And what are you going to tell him when you see him?"

"How do you mean?"

Amelia stared at the floor. Gilli's collection of cuddly toys poked out from under the bed.

"You know what I mean," Gilli said, in a patronizing voice. "Are you going to give him the push?"

"No!" Amelia said, strongly. "Why should I chuck him – just because we had one silly row?"

"That wasn't what I was thinking of," Gilli told her.

"What then?"

Gilli sighed. "Andy could hardly stop talking about you when he was driving me and Rick home last night. He wanted to know all about you – the things you liked doing, who your friends are, what your favourite food is – everything."

Amelia was torn between feeling flattered and feeling embarrassed.

"He asked all this while Rick was there?"

"Rick thought that it was quite funny. He told Andy that he ought to go out with you, that the two of you were ideally suited."

"And you think that too?"

Gilli smiled. "It would be good, wouldn't it, if the four of us could go out places together, as a foursome? Andy's really nice. You said so yourself, when you were trying to set me up with him."

Amelia shook her head. "I hope you told them that I've already *got* a boyfriend, Gilli."

Gilli looked surprised. "How could I, when I didn't know what you'd told Andy? Remember, I'd just watched you giving him a massive kiss for about half an hour!"

"Oh, for crying out loud!" Amelia complained. "It was only a good-night kiss ..." She stumbled over her words. "... a birthday kiss, I mean. I told him I was going out with Kevin."

Amelia tried to remember exactly what she had told Andy.

"According to Andy, you told him that you and Kevin were practically finished. You told him that, if he waited a couple of weeks, you'd go out with him!"

Amelia stared at the floor again. She knew she wouldn't have betrayed Kevin by saying that, but she also knew that people heard what they wanted to hear.

"He must have got the wrong end of the stick," she said, eventually.

Gilli was disappointed.

"Is that what you want me to tell him?" she asked 'That there's no chance of your going out with him?"

Amelia stood up to go. "Don't tell him anything," she said. "It's between him and me. All right?"

Gilli looked miffed. "All right," she said, in a hurt tone of voice.

*　　*　　*

Walking back to the bus stop, Amelia remembered the conversation they'd had in the Body Shop, two weeks before. Gilli said then that it seemed like all three of them could never have a boyfriend at the same time. Was that coming true now? Was she about to lose Kevin? She got off the bus and turned right instead of left. It was gone six. She was going to be late for dinner, but she didn't care. She rang the doorbell.

"He's in his room," Mrs Atkinson told her. "Go on up."

She knocked on his bedroom door. "I told you before," Kevin's voice whined. "I'm not hungry."

Amelia went in. Kevin was sitting on his bed wearing old jeans and a crumpled T-shirt. There were comics spread across the floor and the bed. The Top Forty played softly from his radio.

"Oh," he said. "It's you."

Amelia stood in the doorway, awkwardly. "Yes," she said, "it's me."

Kevin started to clear a space for her on the bed, but she pulled the chair out from beneath his desk and sat on that instead.

"About last night . . ." she said.

Kevin blushed. "I shouldn't have gone off like that," he said. "I'm sorry."

"I'm sorry too. I wanted you there with me."

"I know."

Amelia paused. "I realize that you weren't having that good a time," she said. "This may take longer than we thought."

Kevin nodded. "We're still on trial, are we?" he asked, in a cynical voice.

"As far as everyone else is concerned, yes."

Kevin looked upset. "I don't care about what everybody else thinks. I only care about you."

Amelia was silent. Kevin got up and came over to the desk. She thought that he was going to try and kiss her, but she wasn't feeling amorous. Instead, though, he pulled open the top drawer. "Here, this is for you."

It was a photo of Kevin on a beach somewhere. He was tanned and smiling in a garish pair of swimming trunks. His body looked incredibly child-like, no more than twelve years old.

"Thanks," she said.

"I've got some scissors," he told her. "If you want to cut out the face."

"It's OK," she told him. "I'll do it at home."

There was another long silence. "What happened after I left?" Kevin asked.

"The same as before. A lot of dancing. A bit of drinking. Kissing in corners. Standard party." She paused. "Oh, Gilli found herself a new boyfriend."

Kevin nodded. He wasn't really interested.

"Want to know who it is?"

"Why, do I know him?"

Amelia nodded. "She's going out with Rick."

The look of relief on Kevin's face was plain to see. "I thought he was after you," he said, softly.

"He was," Amelia replied, patiently. "I told him to get lost."

Kevin smiled. "Come and sit here," he asked.

Amelia joined him on the bed. They kissed. Then they kissed again, more passionately. Amelia began to relax. Kevin's love for her was so real, so warm. How could she have doubted it? Still, she was confused – involved, and not involved at the same time. She knew the reason. Amelia felt guilty about the way she felt. In telling Kevin about Rick, she'd been honest, but only to a point. She remembered kissing Andy last night – how big, how strong he'd felt. That was physical, though. It was Kevin she was in love with: adorable, reliable Kevin, who'd never let her down. But part of her said that her relationship with him wasn't real. It was as though they were carrying on the games they'd played as children – she was the doctor, and he was the nurse. He was still a kid, she told herself. And she was legally a woman.

"What's wrong?" Kevin broke away from her.

"Sorry, I ..." Amelia couldn't tell him the truth. She hadn't sorted out what she really felt yet. "I'm late for dinner. My mum and dad will be mad if I don't show up soon."

"Oh. OK."

Kevin showed her to the door. He seemed satisfied that everything was all right again. He offered to walk Amelia home, but she refused. She needed to be alone. Mum and Dad were already eating when she got back. Amelia threw her coat into the cloakroom and took her meal out of the oven. The photo that Kevin had given her lay forgotten in an inside pocket.

17

It was one of those Mondays. Kevin hardly spoke to anyone. All the lessons were boring. Whenever he heard girls laughing or whispering nearby, he assumed that they were talking about him. After all, the story about him leaving Amelia's party early was bound to percolate down to them. But, today, no one spoke directly to Kevin, not even teachers. It was as though they could sense his black mood.

At home time, Kevin got out as quickly as he could, and was one of the first onto the bus. He managed to get his favourite seat near the front. He'd seen Amelia fleetingly during the day, but wanted to see her for a proper talk. As soon as they were alone, he'd tell her – he didn't want any more of this 'trial boyfriend' rubbish. Either she was going out with him, or she wasn't.

The top deck of the bus began to fill up. Kerry Barton tapped him on the shoulder.

"On your own, toy-boy? Want some company?"

Kevin swore at her.

"Ooh! Get him!"

Kevin stared sullenly ahead. He heard the slow, deep tones of Dean Gates.

"What's wrong, Kerry?"

"You should have heard what Kevin told me to do when I offered to sit with him."

Dean laughed. He had an ugly, artificial sort of laugh. The next thing Kevin knew, the huge boy was sitting down next to him.

"Get lost, Dean."

"You were rude to Kerry. She's my friend."

"She was rude to me. Go on, leave it, Dean. I'm waiting for Amelia."

"I heard that Amelia's not coming," Dean said as though he were telling a joke.

"What do you mean?"

"I heard that she threw you out of her party so that she could get off with someone else."

This time, Dean laughed. Kevin got up. He didn't want to lose control.

"That's rubbish, Dean, and you know it. If you won't move, I will."

Dean grabbed the sleeve of Kevin's jacket. "Siddown. I haven't finished with you yet."

"Get off!"

But Dean didn't let go. Kevin was aggravated. He knew that he would regret it later, but he couldn't stop himself. When Dean laughed at him again, Kevin threw the first punch.

Amelia nearly didn't walk all the way upstairs on the bus. As soon as she heard the chants of "Fight, Fight", she started to turn back. But, as she did, all the kids from the lower deck started to throng up the steps behind her to see what was going on. She had to go up or be crushed. At the top of the stairs, Amelia couldn't believe what she saw. Kevin was on the floor, being mauled by Dean Gates. For a few seconds, she could only watch in horror. Dean was twice Kevin's size and didn't fight cleanly. Occasionally, Kevin managed to wriggle away from Dean and land a punch onto his flabby chest, but it had no effect.

"Get off him," Amelia shouted. "Dean, stop that now!"

But Dean ignored her. Behind Amelia, she could hear a bunch of Fourth-Year girls laughing and giggling. Then she heard the voice of Mr Stimson, the teacher on bus duty.

"Break it up! Now!"

Slowly, Dean pulled himself off Kevin, a sly grin on his face.

"Who started it?" Mr Stimson asked.

"He did," Dean replied.

Kevin said nothing. His face was bruised and bloody. Each of his eyes was swollen.

"Both of you get off the bus. I'm taking you to the Head Teacher's office."

As he descended the stairs, Dean gave Amelia a triumphant glance, then held up both his arms like a prize-fighter. There were cheers. Mr Stimson helped Kevin to his feet.

"You're a fool, Kevin," the teacher said, "picking a fight with a thug like him."

Kevin said nothing. Amelia stood at Kevin's side. "I'll come with him. He needs looking after."

Mr Stimson shook his head. "We'll look after him, Amelia. You go home."

Amelia wanted to argue, but Mr Stimson was already helping Kevin down the steps. A minute later, she wished that she had disobeyed her Drama teacher, and got off the bus. For, the moment the bus departed, the chanting began, and didn't stop until she got off the bus.

"Cradle snatcher, cradle snatcher. . ."

It started as a gentle whisper, more of a hiss.

"Cradle snatcher, cradle snatcher. . ."

Then it got louder, until it built up into a shout, almost a roar.

"CRADLE SNATCHER, CRADLE SNAT-CHER!"

Finally, it went quiet. Amelia, holding back the tears that would make her humiliation worse, heaved a sigh of relief. Only then did the hiss start up again.

"Cradle snatcher, c-r-a-d-l-e s-n-a-t-c-h-e-r . . ."

It continued all the way home. The gaps in between the chant got longer, but the chant itself seemed to get louder, crueller. Even when Amelia went downstairs, early, to wait for her stop, the younger kids on the lower deck did the same chant, only louder, and faster. Amelia had to use every ounce of concentration she possessed to stop herself from crying. Off the bus, Amelia ran all the way home and flung herself onto the bed, waiting for Kevin to call when he got home. An hour passed and there was no word. Another hour passed. She had to go round. Mr Atkinson opened the door.

"He's just got out of the bath, but I think he's decent. Go upstairs and have a word, love. I know he wants to see you."

"Thanks."

Kevin was wearing a towelling dressing gown. Both of his eyes were swollen.

"Did you hear any of that row downstairs?" Amelia asked him.

"Every word."

"How could you be so stupid . . ."

Amelia started to cry. Kevin put his hand over hers. "I'm just stupid, I s'pose."

He handed her a tissue. "I'm only fourteen," he said.

Amelia gave him a wry smile. "You'll grow up one day."

He tried to smile back, but his expression was more like despair.

"Will you wait for me?"

Amelia didn't reply. Kevin stared at her for what seemed like forever. Then he said, "You're going to finish with me, aren't you?"

Amelia opened her mouth to explain. Then she looked into his eyes. They looked older, wiser than hers would ever be. This was Kevin, she reminded herself. She didn't have to explain.

"I think we'd better," she said. "Don't you?"

Kevin stood up, and looked out of the window. "You remember that Tom Hanks film 'Big'?" he said, without turning to look at her. "We must have seen that when we were both still at primary school."

Amelia's memories were vague. "Remind me."

"Tom Hanks is this twelve-year-old who turns into a thirty-year-old, and this thirty-year-old woman falls in love with him."

"I remember."

"And even though he's a man he still likes all

the same childish things – you know – toys, comics, computer games – and his girlfriend really likes that in him."

Amelia nodded.

"Then, right at the end of the movie, his girlfriend finds out how old he really is, and takes him home to his mum and dad."

Amelia smiled. Kevin always remembered films better than she did.

"What's the point you're making?"

Kevin turned and looked at her. "Right at the end, when Tom Hanks is walking from the car to his old home, he starts to shrink. He gets out as this six-foot man, but, by the time he gets to the porch he's this tiny, twelve-year-old boy with a man's suit just sort of hanging off him. . ."

Amelia said nothing. Kevin had started to cry. "That's me, isn't it?" he said. "I'm that boy."

He came over and she held him, softly. Both of them were crying now. Amelia stroked his beautiful, golden hair. "I so wanted this to work," she said.

"So did I."

"You won't hate me, will you?"

"Nah." Kevin tried to look cheerful. "I knew the score from the start. You always finish with boys first just to make sure that they don't get bored and finish with you."

Amelia gave him a playful punch.

"Ow!"

He was only pretending to be hurt, she could tell. The real hurt was on the inside, and she had put it there. Amelia stood up.

"I think it might be better if we don't see each

other for a while," she said.

"That's easy," Kevin retorted. "I've been excluded from school for two days, and I'm grounded. After that, well, I'll sit downstairs on the bus if that's what you prefer. Or maybe I'll cycle."

Amelia leant forward to kiss him goodbye. Kevin moved his face, so that her kiss landed on his cheek. Without speaking again, she opened the door and blundered downstairs, tears pouring down her face. At the bottom she heard Kevin's mum call out, "Amelia?" But Amelia ignored her, and ran all the way home.

November

18

Kevin's fifteenth birthday was the worst he could remember. There was nothing much he wanted to do, but his parents insisted that he should celebrate somehow. Kevin chose to go bowling, a thing he hadn't done in years. He took Pete, Martyn and Helen. All three of them had been really supportive after Amelia finished with him, even Helen. She had now been going out with Pete for longer than she had with Kevin.

"Is she getting serious?" Kevin asked Pete, while Helen was in the loo.

"Nah. We're just good mates, really," Pete said. He seemed surprised at the question. "Helen says that's the best way to play it."

Kevin nodded. He was glad that Helen had learnt something from her relationship with him.

The evening went badly. Kevin bowled clumsily, going down the side more often than he knocked over a skittle. Martyn was the best player, but he wasn't good enough to make up for his partner. Helen and Pete beat them easily. By the time they were walking through the New

Town to the bus stop it was bitterly cold. Kevin was bloated with coke and burgers and thoroughly fed up.

"Hey!" Helen said to him, hurriedly. "Do you remember that awful Tom Cruise film I went to see with you? Wasn't that one of the worst films you've ever wasted money on?"

Kevin paused, confused. Helen never referred to the fact that he'd been her first boyfriend. Why was she suddenly rattling on like this in the street? He looked at her, then at Pete. They both had the same nervous, sympathetic look. Instead of replying, Kevin looked round. There, on the other side of the street, queueing up to get into Ritzy's night club, was Amelia. She wasn't alone. Kevin recognized the guy. He'd been at Amelia's sixteenth, and at Paul Sykes's party, too: Andy something or other. He had on an expensive looking coat with a long, wide scarf like university students wore. He was about nine inches taller than Amelia and she was looking up to him with a glow in her eyes that was sickeningly familiar.

"Come on, Kev," Martyn said, softly.

As he watched, the couple kissed. Amelia's arms went up around Andy's neck. Kevin began to shiver.

"Yeah, all right," he said. "I'm coming."

Ten days after Amelia's birthday party, there'd been a small cardboard box waiting for Amelia when she got home from school. Inside the packet was a single red rose. On the side of it was a card.

"I meant what I said.
   X, Andy."

Without taking the flower from its wrapping, Amelia threw the packet into the bin.

"I told him to wait," she said angrily. "I'm not ready for him yet."

But she knew, as she threw scalding water at her face a moment later, that as far as Andy Carrogan and her was concerned, it was only a matter of time.

Two nights later he rang. In a relaxed voice, he asked her out. Amelia didn't hesitate for long.

"This weekend's no good. But if you can be patient, I don't think that I've got anything on next weekend. . ."

"I can be very patient," Andy told her.

And, as it turned out, she had seen him that weekend, when Gilli phoned up and suggested that she joined her and Rick for a drive . . . in Andy's car. They had lunch in a country pub with brasses on the walls and a babbling brook running by outside. It was a much better way to spend Sunday than stuck at home because your boyfriend was watching football with his mates.

"He's really stuck on you," Gilli confided, when the two boys were at the bar. "You ought to put him out of his misery."

"I only split up with Kevin last week."

"But you said that had nothing to do with Andy in the end."

"No. It didn't. Not really."

"So why won't you give Andy a chance now?"

Amelia shrugged. "I told him that I'd probably go out with him next week."

"'Probably'?"

"All right. Definitely."

Gilli smiled. She really wanted for her and Amelia to be able to double date, but Amelia felt awkward. It wasn't just that she wasn't ready for a new boyfriend yet. It was the fact that Gilli was going out with her ex-boyfriend. Why did things have to get so messy? On the way home, Andy dropped off Gilli and Rick first. Amelia was alone with him for the first time since her party. He talked about his exams and asked about hers.

"Six months to go, huh? Are you going to college after school?"

Amelia shook her head. "I did think about doing a performing arts course, but I was kidding myself. I'm not talented enough to be an actress, and I don't have the determination. Anyway, I probably won't get good enough GCSEs to get in."

"Don't run yourself down."

"I'm not. I'm being realistic. I'm not academic. I might be OK at something like office skills, but I'd rather pick them up working in an office."

"But how will you manage that, without qualifications?"

"I've already had offers."

Friends of her dad's had said that if she ever wanted a job, she only had to ask. Amelia could put them to the test, if she wanted. When you were good-looking, doors opened for you. That might be unfair, but life often was unfair. Amelia would take advantage of her looks, however, if anyone tried to treat her as a bimbo, they'd better watch out. Later on – if she found she needed more qualifications – there was day release, or evening classes.

All too quickly, they were outside Amelia's home. Andy parked just beyond the driveway.

"I'd better not ask you in," she said. "I'd have to put up with all sorts of questions."

"That's all right."

He smiled affectionately. He was so confident that his confidence seemed to rub off on her. She felt almost happy for the first time in a fortnight.

"Will I see you next weekend?" he asked.

"Yes," she told him. "Whatever you want to do. Definitely."

Tonight, on their first proper date, he'd taken her to a movie – not to the Odeon, but to one shown on a tiny screen at the college's cinema club – a film with subtitles and endless bare breasts called "Death in a French Garden".

Amelia found it boring. But Andy seemed to enjoy it. The tiny theatre was very dark and almost empty. They moved from hand-holding to cuddling to smooching as the film progressed. Kevin had never done more than hold her hand at the pictures. Rick often acted like he was there on sufferance. Andy, however, seemed to belong in the darkened room, where erotic images buzzed through her head. Afterwards, Andy took her to Ritzy's, a club she'd never been to before, as it was supposed to be for over-21s. They had to queue for twenty minutes in the cold, but Andy kept her warm. When they got to the front of the queue, they had no trouble getting in. They danced until one, the curfew she'd been given for the evening.

Andy was perfect, Amelia decided, as she drifted off to sleep. He was tall, handsome, and intelligent. OK, he was probably going off to university next year and that put a limit on things. But university was eleven months away and anything could happen by then. Look what had happened in the last three weeks: one day she was going out with a handsome, charming fourteen-year-old; the next she had an eighteen-year-old boyfriend who was like the fantasy boys she'd dreamt of when she was a kid.

Only Kevin wasn't fourteen any more, was he? Amelia remembered with a horrible stab of guilt that today was his birthday – four weeks to the day after hers. And she hadn't even sent him a card. How could she have been so cruel? It was unforgivable. When they were still going out, she had planned to buy him a watch. That seemed too extravagant now. But Kevin had spent a lot of money buying her the locket which was now tucked away in her bottom drawer.

Ages later, still unable to sleep, Amelia remembered that she had a Boots voucher that her aunt and uncle had given her for her birthday. She hadn't used it yet. It was an impersonal present, but maybe that was the best kind at the moment. Kevin could use it to buy a computer game.

Although it was nearly three in the morning, she got out of bed and found the voucher. It had come inside a card and didn't have anything written on it. All she had to do was buy a card tomorrow and deliver it in the morning. Then she would only be a day late. If she timed it right, there was no chance of bumping into Kevin, either. She wasn't ready for that yet.

When Kevin got back from his paper round that Sunday morning there was a message for him to ring Paul Sykes. He hadn't spoken to Karen's boyfriend since Amelia's birthday party. They weren't exactly friends, though they got on well enough. Kevin had no idea what the older boy might want. He rang him. There were no pleasantries.

"You're a useful football player, aren't you?"

"S'pose."

Kevin played centre half for the Fourth-Year boys team and for a Saturday morning team too.

"Thing is. . . I'm captain of the estate mixed league side and we've got half our team down with flu. D'you think you could turn out for us today? It's a home game."

Kevin had nothing better to do. "All right."

"Kick-off's at twelve. Be at the leisure centre for half eleven."

"I'll see you there."

Kevin arranged for his dad to give him a lift later, then got in an extra hour's kip. When he came downstairs, there was an envelope on the doormat bearing his name, in achingly familiar writing. That was what he and Amelia had come to – a measly birthday card a day late. Without opening the envelope, Kevin tore the card in two and put it into the bin.

On the way to the game, his father ribbed him about playing in a mixed game.

"Not too much of the kissing and cuddling when you score, now. And what about the showers afterwards, eh?"

"Oh, get lost, Dad."

The team, as it turned out, wasn't very mixed. There were eight girls to three boys, with no sub. The opposition only had two boys.

"Problem is," Paul explained to Kevin, "we can only get lads who can't manage a regular game any other way. Then, when they find out that the girls are loads better than them, they don't come back."

Kevin nodded. He looked around while Paul discussed team tactics. There were a couple of girls he recognized who used to go to Westtown Comp, but most of the faces were unfamiliar. Paul told him that they went to St Theresa's, the Catholic school several miles away.

"Remember me?" a tall girl with blonde hair asked as they warmed up on the icy pitch.

"Uh . . . yeah," Kevin struggled.

She was a fresh-faced, attractive girl, who looked familiar. But seeing her in soccer kit, without make-up, disorientated him. Then he remembered who he'd seen her with.

"Tracey, isn't it?"

Tracey nodded. "We met at Paul's party. You're Kevin aren't you? You were with a girl called Amelia."

"That's right. But not any more. We split."

Now Kevin remembered who Tracey had been with. "In fact, I think she's going out with that guy you were with. Andy."

Tracey frowned. "Really? In that case, I'm sorry for her."

"Why?"

"She'll find out."

19

The only drag about going out with Andy was that he worked a lot. He needed at least three B grades if he was to study Law at university. When Amelia maintained that she intended to leave school the next year, it clearly disturbed him. Amelia began to have second thoughts. She even found herself working harder at school, because she thought that Andy would respect her more if she did. Her grades improved a little, just in time for the Fifth-Year parents' evening. Mum and Dad were delighted.

"See what you can do," Mum told her, "with a bit of hard work. They all say the same thing. It's not too late for you to get good grades if you really try."

Amelia's teachers had been despairing of her for years.

"You know," Dad told her, "it's not impossible that you could get to a university yourself – if you made up your mind that it was what you really wanted to do."

"Oh, *come on*," Amelia said, "I'd hate it – more

years of essays and exams. And you end up thousands of pounds in debt if you're a student these days. No, thank you."

"There's the social life too," Mum went on. "I remember meeting your father during my second term. . ."

"Stop, *please*," Amelia told her. "I really don't need reminding what a wonderful time you both had at Reading. I have a perfectly good social life at the moment."

"Yes, but how long will it last?" Mum asked.

"It'll probably improve when I get a job and have more money to spend," Amelia snapped back.

"But what kind of job will you get with just a few GCSEs?" Dad wanted to know.

"That's enough!" Amelia annnounced. "I've had it up to here!"

She stormed upstairs to her room, vowing never again to hand her homework in on time, not if this was the reward it brought her. A few good marks, and Mum and Dad wanted to change her whole personality. Amelia would have liked to ring up Andy and have a good moan, but she didn't think he'd understand. No point in ringing Gilli, either. Gilli loved school. She was already having fantasies about following Rick to Portsmouth when she'd done her "A" levels.

Kevin always understood. He saw school as a means to an end – something you got through, then got out of. Amelia still found herself thinking about Kevin a lot. Her time with him had been a necessary healing period, she thought. It had helped her work out what she most valued in a relationship. Every time Amelia thought about

Kevin her feelings became confused. She felt guilty about the way she'd treated him, angry too, about the way it had worked out. Mainly, though, she felt frustrated. Part of her, she was sure, was still in love with him, and felt like it always would be. But she wasn't sure what sort of love it was. How many were there? Maybe it could never have worked in the long term because Kevin was far too young. Amelia wasn't sure about that. The thing she was sure about was that, one day, they would be able to be friends again.

But not yet. If she rang him up out of the blue, how would he react? Bitterness, probably. Resentment. Or, worse, he might think that she wanted to get back together with him. Amelia reached into the Indian rucksack she used for school and pulled out a packet of Marlboros. Her parents hated it when she smoked in the house. They had both given up twenty years ago. Well, tough. This was her room, and she'd do what she wanted to do in it. Tonight, she wasn't the soft, dreamy girl who Kevin had fallen in love with. She was older and more mature. She was hard.

Amelia closed the copy of *Great Expectations* that she was meant to be reading for English. Then she got a tabloid paper out of her bag instead. "Air Steward tells of sizzling affair with Argentinian Ice Skater!" That was all she felt like reading tonight. Sometimes, she was so fed up with life in this small village, surrounded by the same old people, with their small minds. Maybe she'd become an air stewardess herself, fly away from the lot of them.

*   *   *

"Kevin! Over here!"

Kevin charged across the hard pitch, looking for space to pass Tracey the ball. She was in a good position, clear to the left of goal, not quite off-side. Kevin had one player to get clear of first. The opposition central defender was built like a battering ram. But this meant that she was slow, and should be easy to get past. Kevin ran straight at the defender, then did a neat body swerve to shuffle around her. He launched the ball towards Tracey.

"Ow!"

The defender's bulky leg caught Kevin just as he released the ball, sending him crashing onto the frozen ground. His ankle was in such agony that he barely registered the cries of "goal!" from other members of the Estate team. Tracey had scored.

"Ah, c'mon ref! We thought you'd given a foul on their other striker."

"Rubbish! He played the advantage."

"Hey, is Kevin all right?"

The last voice was Tracey's. She came running over to where Kevin lay on the ground, clutching his ankle.

"How bad is it?"

"I'll be OK. I fell awkwardly, that's all. Did the goal stand?"

"The goal stood," Tracey told him, with concern in her voice. "But I'm not sure if you will. Come on. Let me help you up."

She put an arm under Kevin's shoulder and he put his around her. Slowly, she lifted him to his feet. He was in agony. The referee came over and examined Kevin's ankle.

"A bad twist," he told him. "You'll be over it in a day or two."

Tracey helped Kevin limp to the sideline. The game was interrupted for ten minutes while the referee bandaged Kevin up. When they played on, Tracey's goal proved the decider. The Estate team won 3-2.

Tracey came over and sat with Kevin after the game. "Paul's gone to ring your dad, see if he can fetch you," she told him.

Kevin thanked her.

"But what am I going to do about my bike?"

"I'll take it if you like," Tracey said, "ride it over for you later."

"Are you sure?"

Tracey nodded. "Of course I'm sure. Anyway, you made my goal. I owe you. Where do you live?"

Tracey was as good as her word. Four hours later she was at the house with Kevin's bike.

"How's the ankle?"

Kevin shrugged. "I've had worse injuries. Looks like I'll have to miss my paper round for a couple of days though."

Tracey smiled sympathetically. "Don't suppose you can dance, either. Pity. There's this all-night rave I was going to ask you to take me to tonight."

Kevin grinned. "Some other time."

"OK," Tracey told him. "Some other time."

She stayed for half an hour. They talked about sport, mainly. Tracey seemed to know everything there was to know about every sport that Kevin had heard of, as well as one or two that he hadn't.

Eventually, the subject of Tracey's ex-boyfriend came up.

"And which sport was Andy into?" Kevin asked.

Tracey's expression turned sour. "Only one," she said. "And when I told him he wasn't going to play it with me, that was when we parted ways."

The sarcasm in her voice turned into anger. "I hate his type," she said. "I've met a few of them – well-off lads from the village who think they're God's gift. They seem really nice at first. But you soon find out how they operate. They think that if they pick up a girl from the Council Estate, they can do what they want with them. I told him to get lost."

Kevin nodded. He wondered if Amelia would do the same thing.

On Monday morning, Amelia decided to stop off at the newsagents before she caught the school bus. She was out of cigarettes. She opened the door of the shop and was almost at the counter when she saw who was standing in front of it. Kevin was saying "I think I should be all right for tomorrow."

Then he turned to go and noticed Amelia. His face clouded over.

"Why aren't you doing your round?" she asked.

Kevin mumbled. "Did my ankle in, playing football. Got to catch the bus today."

Amelia forced a smile. Now that she had bumped into Kevin, she couldn't just walk away. "All right if I come with you?"

"If you like."

As Amelia followed Kevin out, the newsagent

called to Amelia. "Didn't you want something?"

"It doesn't matter," Amelia said.

Theirs was only the second stop, so the bus was nearly empty. They had the top deck to themselves. "How's things?" Amelia asked.

Kevin shrugged. "Not bad."

"Are you going out with anyone?" Amelia asked.

"Not at the moment."

The reply pleased Amelia, though she knew that it shouldn't. They lapsed into an awkward silence. Kevin wanted to know how she was getting on with Andy, whether he behaved with Amelia as he had with Tracey. But he didn't know how to phrase the question. He'd rather believe the worst. More people got onto the bus as it travelled towards the school. There were no comments about Kevin sitting with Amelia. It was common knowledge that she was going out with someone else. Over the last month, Kevin had become really fed up of people telling him where they'd seen Amelia, and with whom. In fact, it had occurred to him to date one of the girls in his year, purely in order to get the gossips off his back. But most of the Fourth-Year girls were still down on him and, anyway, girls his own age seemed really immature now. They bored him. It was funny how, when you were forced to view people from a distance, they became less interesting.

"What are you thinking about?"

Amelia's voice was tender, as though they were still together. Kevin snapped to attention. "Nothing much."

Amelia frowned. "It's too early, isn't it?"

"Too early for what?"

"For us to be friends again."

Kevin shook his head. "It's not too early," he told her. "It's too late."

Amelia didn't reply. A moment later, she got out a hankie and began to rub her face. Kevin didn't look round, so he couldn't tell whether she was crying, or merely had something in her eye.

December

20

"Anyway," said Tracey, "the thing is, do I stay on at St Theresa's next autumn, or do I go to the Sixth-Form college in the new town?"

"I dunno," said Kevin, smiling, "does it make all that much difference?"

Tracey gave him a funny look. Then she leant forward and kissed him. "You know it does," she said, when they'd finished. "I need to know what you're doing."

Kevin tried to decide how to tell her. They'd been playing football together for five weeks now. Despite the ankle injury, he hadn't missed a game. Kevin and Tracey were the team's top scorers. They'd been out together twice. Kevin hadn't really been looking for a girlfriend, but Tracey was comfortable to be with. And, for some reason, she was dead keen on him. Kevin had assumed that Tracey knew how old he was. One of the girls from his school must have told her, or Paul Sykes. But she didn't seem to.

"Are you going to stay on next year? Or are you going to try to get a job?" Tracey asked.

Kevin prevaricated. "I haven't really thought about Sixth-Form yet," he told her. "It's a long way off. I mean, I think I'd prefer a job, but they're hard to come by at the moment. I'll see what the situation's like when I finish school."

"But that's only six months away," Tracey told him.

Then she paused. Worry lines spread across her face. "I'm missing something here, aren't I? You don't expect to be going out with me in six months, do you?"

Kevin put an arm around her. "It's not that. It's just . . ."

Tracey shook her head. "Don't bother explaining."

She stared bitterly out of the cafe window. "You know, something like this always happens when I start to care about someone. Either he's not really interested in me, or he's only interested in me for one thing. I thought you were different."

"It's not what you think," Kevin protested.

Tracey shook her head. She turned to face him.

"Forget it," she said. "I over-reacted. Just promise you won't dump me before Christmas. I already bought your present."

Kevin smiled. "I won't dump you if you don't dump me," he said. "But there's something you ought to know."

Tracey still looked concerned. "What?"

"The reason that Sixth-Form college is a long way off."

He nearly stumbled over the words. "I'm in the Fourth Year."

Tracey looked confused. "You got put back a year?"

"No. I only just turned fifteen."

Tracey shrugged. "And I thought . . ."

She leant forward and kissed him again. "How old's Amelia?"

"Same age as you."

Tracey smiled. "First her, now me . . . so you prefer older women, do you?"

Kevin laughed. "It's beginning to look that way."

"Come on," she said. "I thought we were going to watch the satellite match round at your mate's house."

They got up and walked to the bus stop, hand in hand.

"We've been going out for over a month. You know I'm serious about you!"

"If you're serious then you'll wait until I'm ready."

"What do you think I have been doing? Most blokes . . ."

"I don't *care* what most blokes would do. I want it to happen when it feels right, not just because we happen to have the house to ourselves . . ."

Andy smiled. "It sounds like the ideal time to me."

Amelia moved away from him. She was confused. One minute she thought that she was falling in love. The next she barely recognized her boyfriend. How come a few drinks transformed an intelligent, warm guy into someone with a one-track mind?

"You'll have to be patient with me," she told him. "It's just that. . ."

Andy interrupted. "I respect you, Amelia. If you're not ready for something, you're not ready. But I want to tell you something. I've never said this to a girl before and it scares me. I love you. And that's why I want. . ."

"Ssssh."

Amelia kissed him. She was being stupid, holding out like this. Andy was the best thing that had ever happened to her. She knew, and Andy knew, that Gilli was sleeping with Rick. She'd only been going out with him a fortnight longer than Amelia had been seeing Andy. Maybe tonight *was* the night. . .Amelia kissed Andy again, more tenderly this time. Andy stroked her back. With his other hand, he was reaching into his pocket for something. Amelia could guess what it was. Andy was responsible.

"Mmmm," she murmured, "that feels good."

Andy wasn't like Rick. He took things slowly, making up for his earlier clumsiness. Even so, as they got nearer to the point of no return, Amelia felt uncomfortable. *This doesn't feel right*, she told herself. *I shouldn't feel scared.*

"Wait," she said, softly. "Not yet."

"I can't wait," Andy whispered urgently. "What's wrong with you? It's not as if it's the first time. Rick told me. . ."

Amelia froze. She pushed Andy off her. "If Rick told you anything like that, he was lying," she said, loudly.

"OK. OK. I shouldn't have mentioned it. I'm sorry."

"So am I. I'm sorry that you believed him. It makes me wonder whether I should believe you – 'I've never said this to a girl before' – some people will say anything they think a girl wants to hear if they think she'll give them what they want."

"I'm not like that," Andy said, angrily.

Amelia gave him a long, hard look. "Then you're going to have to prove it," she told him, "however long it takes."

Slowly, Andy nodded his head. "OK."

"OK," Amelia said. "Now it's late. I think it's time for you to go."

Andy gave her a surly look. Then he did as he was told.

The funny thing was, several girls at school knew that Kevin was going out with Tracey, but none of them teased him about it. Maybe it was because she didn't go to Westtown Comp. Moreover, Pete and Martyn both liked her, and she got on well with Helen, too. The only thing that Kevin found odd about Tracey was the way that she was sport obsessed – not just football, but netball, hockey, badminton, swimming and, in summer she warned him, tennis. She had so many games and practices that it was hard to see a lot of her.

But when he didn't see Tracey, it wasn't like the times that he couldn't see Amelia. That had felt like a real ache, something gnawing away at his heart. Being with Tracey had stopped him hurting for Amelia so much. Not being with her wasn't a pain though. It was more like an itch that he couldn't scratch. Kevin never saw Amelia now. If he passed her in a corridor, he would look the other way, if she hadn't done so first. Since the awkward encounter in the newsagents the previous month, he'd taken to cycling to and from school, even when the weather was lousy. It meant he didn't have to see her on the bus going home, get off at the same stop as her.

There was one daily reminder though. Every morning, the last paper he delivered before returning home was to her house. He hadn't changed his route since they split up. Her curtains were always closed, and he didn't suppose that she had any idea he came to her last. He'd never told her. One of these days, he often told himself, he'd ask to change his round. But he never remembered to do it.

A week before Christmas, Amelia sent Kevin a card. It was a funny one: a little girl was talking to her mother, who was washing dishes,

"Why are your hands so soft, Mummy?"

The mother removes a limp hand from the soap water and replies, "Because I've had all the bones taken out!"

Inside, Amelia had written, "Don't be a stranger. Come on Boxing Day. Love, A."

On Boxing Day, Amelia's parents held open house. Friends from the village came round for a drink, mince pies and conversation. Kevin had been going round to the Gormans' on Boxing Day for as long as he could remember. But he hadn't been inside the house since the night of Amelia's birthday party. Kevin wasn't sure he could face it. Also, he was hoping to see Tracey that day. He wasn't keen on taking her round there, especially since Amelia was going out with Tracey's ex-boyfriend.

On Saturday, Kevin bought Tracey's present, the new Madonna CD. He used the money he had left to buy himself a T-shirt. Tracey had hinted that he needed some new casual clothes for the festive season. They had a double date that night, a rock concert in Birmingham. Tracey's dad had generously offered to drive them there and visit friends while they were at the concert. The other couple going to the concert were Paul and Karen. Paul and Tracey were friends, but Kevin had hardly seen Karen since Amelia's party.

"You've grown!" was the first thing she told him.

It was true. He was in the middle of a growth spurt, and had put on nearly two inches in just over two months.

"You haven't."

Karen was still four ten, while Paul was nearly six feet tall. They looked an odd couple, but seemed happy together. Kevin asked after Karen's best friend. Immediately he'd finished speaking, he sensed that he'd asked the wrong question.

"Gilli's still totally obsessed with Rick Jones. I never see her outside school any more. Amelia does. Her and Andy go out with the two of them. But me and Paul. . ."

"We're not good enough for them," Paul interrupted. "Those two act like they're at university already."

"They're creeps," Karen agreed. "I don't know why Gilli or Amelia . . ."

"Oh, please," interrupted Tracey, who was in the front seat, "Amelia, Amelia – do you have to keep mentioning her name?"

Paul and Karen stopped talking. *She knows*, Kevin thought. Tracey knows that I'm still stuck on Amelia. He kept thinking about this during the concert, which wasn't much good. Their seats were so far away that they'd have got a better view watching it on television. Tracey was much better suited to Kevin than Amelia was. They had more interests in common. Kevin found Tracey really attractive. And she was really keen on him. But it still wasn't enough.

On the way home, even Paul found it hard to work up enthusiasm for the concert they'd just been to. He sat in the front, while Tracey and Kevin cuddled in the back. Karen fell asleep, or pretended to.

"I'm looking forward to Christmas," Tracey whispered, gently.

"Me too."

"We'll be able to spend lots of time together."

"Yeah."

He squeezed her tighter. Neither of them had mentioned the promise which Kevin had made a few days before. He would go out with Tracey until Christmas. After that, there were no guarantees. The way he saw it, the school holidays were a kind of make or break. Either he and Tracey became closer, and he cast off the spectre of Amelia Gorman, or they didn't, and they ought to call it quits. It wouldn't be fair to Tracey to drag it out. But he didn't discuss any of this with Tracey. He'd never been as open about his feelings to her as he'd been able to be with Amelia. Instead, Kevin thanked Tracey's father when he dropped him off, and kissed Tracey chastely on the lips.

"Sleep well. I'll see you at the match tomorrow."

She smiled as if to tell him she'd say a lot more if her father wasn't there. Kevin forced a smile back. It was no good. He was beginning to feel the way he felt when Helen Scott told him that she loved him. He wanted to put up a "Slow" sign. Or maybe even one reading "Stop!"

21

Andy's Christmas present for Amelia was a necklace – a simple, gold-plated chain with a heart pendant on the end of it. It was an unfortunate choice, but Andy didn't know about the one that Kevin had given her, which she never wore. Unlike Kevin's, this heart didn't open. There was no message engraved on it. Perhaps Andy had thought, up to the last moment, that Amelia would drop him. Then he would have saved it for another girl.

Over the last two months, Gilli had become Amelia's best friend, instead of Karen's. Not that the other two girls had fallen out. But Karen had Paul now, and Amelia had lost Kevin. She needed Gilli's friendship more. And, most significantly, they were dating boys who were best friends.

"Can Gilli come to the phone?"

"I'll see, Amelia. She's not too well," Gilli's mum replied. "Gilli!"

"What's wrong with her?" Amelia asked.

"She's coming, so she can tell you herself."

Amelia heard her friend's footsteps. From her

breathy 'hello' it was obvious that she'd been crying.

"Gilli, what happened?"

"It's Rick. He's chucked me."

"At Christmas? How could he?"

The words tumbled out breathlessly. "He met someone at the college end-of-term party last week. He says he prefers her to me and it wouldn't be fair to lie about it."

Amelia called Rick a few choice names. She'd known about the end-of-term party. Andy said that he'd "looked in" on it. He said he didn't ask Amelia because he knew how boring she'd find it.

"You know what Rick told me?" Gilli went on. "He said that I was 'a bit young' for him, that he preferred to be with someone his own age."

Amelia sighed. She remembered the advice that Gilli had given her a few months ago, when she was going out with Rick. It had proved accurate, but it was Gilli who it had happened to. Rick had got what he wanted from her, then got bored, and cast her off. For the next half hour, Amelia agreed with her friend about how rotten men were, how, most of the time, they were better off without them.

Gilli's news cast a pall over the rest of Christmas Day. Andy had been round for half an hour in the morning, to exchange presents (she had given him a stylish watch, with a completely blank, black face and luminous hands – he said he loved it). He wasn't coming again. After dinner, when everyone was crashed out in front of the movie, Amelia went for a walk on her own.

Normally, any other year, she would have

called in on Kevin. But she hadn't spoken to him for what seemed like months, not since the horrible conversation they'd had on the bus to school. It was cold. She stuffed her hands in her pockets and walked past the end of his street, without looking down it. She felt something crinkle in the lining of her anorak and reached into the inside pocket. Amelia pulled out a crumpled photograph that she had completely forgotten – it was Kevin, on a beach somewhere. It was probably taken this year, but he looked much younger than he did now. It seemed like every time she saw him lately, he had grown another inch and his face had become more serious.

Now that she was well beyond Kevin's street, Amelia glanced back. As if on cue, a familiar bicycle turned the corner. Kevin, wearing his Bell Image helmet, didn't see her. He rode in the opposite direction. For a moment, Amelia thought that he might be coming to see her. But, at the end of the road, he turned left, towards the new town. Who could he be going to see on Christmas afternoon? Amelia walked on. She missed Kevin. She missed his company. He was so easy to be with. There was never any pressure from Kevin. And she trusted him completely, a way she didn't trust Andy, with all his charm and front and foreign films. Soon, Andy would be gone, to a world where she couldn't follow. No matter what he said, Andy wasn't serious about her. But Kevin was. . .

Or he had been. Amelia tried to remember what she had let tear them apart – the teasing, the jealousy, the petty hatreds of immature schoolchildren – nothing that anyone should take seriously. But she had. And, for a while, it seemed like there'd been somebody better waiting in the wings. She might have known that he would turn out to have feet of clay. Or maybe he didn't. Maybe Andy was pretty good, as boyfriends went. In which case, what she had with Kevin was unique.

It was too late now, Amelia realized. If she and Kevin were going to get together again, it was in the distant future, when they were old enough to look back at all this and laugh. But it was too late for her and Andy, too. She'd never loved him, really. She doubted that he was really in love with her. He was fun to be with, but she wasn't going to sleep with someone she wasn't in love with. Once she told him that, he'd walk. So she might as well pack him in first.

Kevin mentioned Boxing Day afternoon at Amelia's casually, like he wasn't bothered about it. "We don't have to go," he said, "in fact, if we stay here, we'll probably have the place to ourselves, because my mum and dad are going."

Tracey shrugged. "It might be interesting to pop in for half an hour."

"Why?"

Tracey gave a wicked grin. "Revenge. Show Andy and Amelia that both of us are better off without them."

Kevin laughed awkwardly. He'd been afraid she might take that attitude.

"Also," Tracey went on, "I think you need to get this Amelia out of your system. You told me that you agreed to split up with her, but whenever I mention her name, your face goes all doomy. Were you telling the truth? Or did she dump you?"

Kevin thought for a moment. "We agreed to split up," he said, "and it was my fault as much as hers. But I knew that, if I hadn't agreed, she'd have chucked me anyway. So I guess it feels like she did chuck me, even though she didn't, if you see what I mean."

Tracey nodded. "I think so. In that case, I think we should definitely go round there tomorrow. I know Andy Carrogan and, believe me, I got the better end of the deal. We'll show her what she's missing!"

At two on Boxing Day afternoon, Kevin and Tracey walked over to the Gormans' with Kevin's mum and dad. Tracey chattered cheerfully. Kevin was sure that they were making a mistake. But he did want to see Amelia. It had been too long. Mr Gorman let them in. The large house was full of adults. Amelia was nowhere to be seen. The only person her age who Kevin could spot was her friend Gilli. She was hovering at the bottom of the stairs, so he went over and said hello to her. Gilli looked miserable.

"Karen not with you?"

"I've hardly seen her recently."

Kevin remembered Karen suggesting that the two of them had drifted apart, so he didn't pursue the question.

"Do you remember Tracey?"

Gilli didn't, so Kevin was busy explaining who

she was when someone hurried down the stairs behind them. Kevin looked round. It was Andy Carrogan. He didn't look happy.

"Hello, Andy," Tracey said, sweetly. "Do you remember Kevin?"

Andy gave Tracey a horrible look. Then, ignoring them, he began digging through the coats piled up on the end of the banister. Finding the one he wanted, he yanked it out, then pushed through the adults to the open front door. There, he paused, took the watch off his wrist, threw it onto the floor and stamped on.it. Two minutes later, Amelia came down the stairs. She looked perfectly calm. Indeed, Kevin thought, she looked quite beautiful. She had on the white silk top he knew so well. The smile she gave him was familiar, too. Kevin's heart did two flip-flops. He knew he shouldn't have come.

"Has he gone?" Amelia asked Gilli.

"Yes. He's gone."

Gilli pointed to the watch on the floor. Amelia picked it up. The face was broken. "I've got the receipt," she told them. "Do you think I could still persuade them to change it for me?"

Kevin laughed nervously. He could see the anxiety on Amelia's face as she went off to the kitchen. She was on the verge of bursting into tears. But she had dumped Andy Carrogan. That much was clear.

"This is Tracey," he said, as Amelia returned with a tray full of drinks.

"I think we met at Paul Sykes's party," Tracey said, politely.

Amelia blinked. "You used to go out with Andy?"

"That's right."

Amelia was drinking bacardi and coke, not her normal drink. Kevin didn't comment, though he knew that her parents never let her have anything stronger than wine. She took a big gulp of it and did a double take at Tracey.

"And now you go out with Kevin?"

"That's right," Tracey said.

Amelia smiled in a goofy way which made her teeth look horsey. "We swapped," she said, as though she was talking to herself.

Tracey nodded politely. "I guess we kind of did."

Amelia downed the rest of her drink. "Want to swap back?"

Tracey nearly choked on her orange juice. She didn't know how to react. Kevin laughed and tried to make a joke of it. "Good old Amelia – goes mad with any bloke who treats a girl like a possession, but it's perfectly all right for a girl to treat a boy that way. Isn't that right?"

"I don't know," Amelia said. "That was too complicated for me. Is it?"

She held out her empty glass for him to refill. Kevin was glad to get away. He went to the kitchen and poured her a glass full of coke. If Amelia got any more drunk, she might well go over the top. As he started to make his way back to her, Mr Gorman tapped him on the shoulder.

"It's good to see you here, Kevin. We've missed having you around."

Kevin smiled bashfully.

"How's school?"

Kevin shrugged. He wanted to get back to Amelia, but was forced to make polite conversation for five minutes. When he got away, the group of three girls was nowhere to be seen. Nor were their drinks around. Wherever Amelia had gone, she had taken his cider with her. He looked outside. No one in the garden. They must be upstairs. Normally, he'd have gone up there. But, at a party like this, it would look a bit strange, his striding upstairs to a girl's bedroom. So he stayed put. They'd be back in a minute.

Half an hour later, Kevin was bored out of his wits. He was good at conversation with adults, but they rarely had anything interesting to say to him. He kept glancing up the stairs. More people were leaving the party than arriving. Soon, his mum and dad would be going. He'd hoped to go home with Tracey before them, to have some time in the house alone. Finally, he'd had enough. He went up the stairs as though he was going to the bathroom. The first sounds he heard were howls of laughter coming from Amelia's room. He knocked on the door. He could hear Amelia saying: "And the way he always looks at himself in every mirror he passes . . ."

"Oh, I know. . ." Tracey said.

The girls laughed even louder. Kevin knocked again. "What!" Amelia shouted impatiently.

Kevin pushed the door open. The three girls were sitting on the floor with their shoes off and empty glasses in front of them. Amelia was smoking.

"Eh . . . it's getting kind of lonely downstairs," Kevin muttered.

"Sorry, Kevin, it's girl talk," Tracey said,

suppressing a giggle. "We're slagging off our ex-boyfriends."

"So I gathered."

"Oh, I've got no secrets from Kevin," Amelia announced loudly. "He's the only boy who ever loved me for myself."

Even though Kevin knew that she was drunk, Amelia's words made his heart spin. He found himself making excuses for her. She was upset. She wasn't herself. But, as the girls carried on their conversation, Kevin got embarrassed. He didn't want to hear about how slimy Andy Carrogan had turned out to be. Tracey squeezed his hand. It felt uncomfortable, all wrong, for her to be holding his hand in front of Amelia. As soon as he could, without being obvious, Kevin took his hand away. Eventually, Tracey noticed how bored he was, and suggested that they go. Amelia stood, too.

"You don't mind if I give your boyfriend a Christmas kiss?" she asked Tracey, slurring the last word.

"Be my guest."

Neither girl asked Kevin. He let Amelia smother him. Her kiss was wet and smokey. It tasted like closing time in a pub. Kevin said good-bye and got out as quickly as he could. Downstairs, nearly everybody had gone.

"She's really nice," Tracey told Kevin. "You've obviously got excellent taste in girlfriends."

Kevin said nothing. He hadn't wanted to be around the Amelia he'd seen this afternoon – high on alcohol and pretending to be more cynical and hard-bitten than she really was. Tracey looked pleased with herself. She thought that Amelia had shown herself up. She thought that the other girl was less of a threat to her now. Yet, when Kevin put Tracey next to Amelia, he still wanted to be with Amelia more. Much more. He knew what he had to do.

22

Amelia woke at three. Her head felt like it was being attacked by a battering ram. She knew straight away that she had only herself to blame. That was it. She was giving up alcohol. Forever. And cigarettes too. Her mouth felt like an ashtray. She remembered how it had happened. She'd had a couple of drinks with Andy while she worked up the nerve to finish with him. He'd been angrier and much more violent than she'd expected. Then she'd had a big drink to get over his storming out. She vaguely remembered making a fool of herself in front of Kevin. She'd been so jealous, seeing him with his new girlfriend.

When they'd gone, she continued getting drunk with Gilli, "celebrating" their freedom. That was how alcoholics began, Amelia thought. In some countries, they didn't let you drink legally until you were twenty-one. Maybe they had it right. Amelia vaguely remembered how the afternoon ended. At six, Amelia's dad drove Gilli home. Mum had no sympathy over Amelia splitting up with Andy. It seemed like she had dumped one boyfriend too many. As she'd cleared out the debris from Amelia's bedroom, Mum gave her only daughter the full lecture. Amelia was a silly, selfish girl who wasn't mature enough to be treated as an adult. She wouldn't be allowed to drink at home again until she was eighteen. On her way out, Mum crushed Amelia's last few cigarettes and put them in the bin.

By four, Amelia was sure that she wouldn't get any more sleep. She dragged herself to the bathroom. She got two panadols out of the cabinet, broke them in half, and poured water onto them. While she was waiting for the pills to dissolve, she tried to remember what day it was. The day after Boxing Day. Sunday. Then she drank the fizzing water, even the crumbly bits at the bottom. After a while, her head began to clear. Amelia remembered something. She went to the bottom drawer of her dresser and took out a silver pendant and chain. It wasn't as expensive as the one that she had returned to Andy, but it was worth a lot more. She got out the photograph that she had found in her pocket on Christmas Day. It was crumpled, but Kevin's face was undamaged. Amelia drew around it with a pencil, then cut the shape out. It was a perfect fit. A moment later, she was wearing Kevin next to her heart. One day, she said to herself. *One day I'll get him back.* But she knew it wouldn't be today. She didn't remember all of yesterday very well, but she remembered that he and Tracey looked right together. And Amelia had really liked Tracey. She wouldn't want to hurt her. One thought stayed with her: the more the girls talked yesterday afternoon, the more they'd slagged off just about every boy they'd ever come into intimate contact with, the more Amelia had realized: Kevin was the one for her. One day, he'd be hers again. He had to be.

Kevin woke at six-thirty. The worst thing about holidays was that they ended. Then you had to get up early to deliver the papers again. And Kevin had slept badly. Tracey had taken it well, all things considered, but Kevin had still felt guilty about it.

"It's not fair to you," he'd told her. "I wish I was in love with you, but I'm not."

Tracey cried. She blamed herself. "I should never have got you to go round there this afternoon."

"But what you said was right," Kevin told her. "I need to get Amelia out of my system before I can go out with somebody else properly."

He paused, then added, "But I haven't been able to do it yet. I'm sorry."

Tracey shook her head and began to cry.

"I can't pretend," Kevin told her.

Kevin's dad drove her home. No one spoke in the car. Without being told, Dad seemed to have sensed what had happened. Kevin walked Tracey to the door.

"You'll be round there, won't you? Tomorrow you'll be with your precious Amelia."

"Maybe," he said, "if she'll have me."

"Oh, she'll have you all right," Tracey said, with a hint of bitterness, "but I wouldn't be sure that it'll last, or even that it'll be good for you while it does."

"I know," Kevin told her. "But I have to find out."

"And if you show up for another game of football," Tracey warned him, "I'll break both your legs!"

Kevin got back into the car. He'd got off lightly, again.

Was Tracey right? Would Amelia go out with him? He didn't know. If Amelia was wise, she wouldn't. They had too much history together. There was too much that they had to get over. But he couldn't keep away from her, all the same. Amelia Gorman was everything he'd ever wanted. It would be hard to make it last, he knew that. He was too young to give her all the things she wanted. Amelia was too selfish and too impatient and far too beautiful for her own good. But she was the one for him. If he didn't go after her while he had the chance, he'd regret if for the rest of his life.

It was a cold, dark morning as Kevin finished his round. Hers was the last house, as usual. Kevin was early this morning. It was barely seven-thirty. There was a small light coming from the hall, which wasn't normally on. It was curious. He would have expected the Gormans to be sleeping in. As Kevin thrust the newspaper through their letter box, the door opened.

"Kevin?"

Amelia stood there in her chinese silk dressing gown. Her face was pale, as though she'd been crying, or was ill.

"Can you come in?"

Kevin pushed his bike into the porch and shut the door behind him. Then he took off his cycle helmet.

"I've been waiting for you," she said. "I wasn't sure what time you'd come, so I've been standing by this door since six o'clock."

Kevin stood facing her in the hallway. It was still dark, except for the small light by the telephone table. A book was open beneath the light. Some old novel. Amelia looked afraid of something. Kevin wanted to kiss her, but he wanted her to know that it was all right first, that he wasn't cheating on anyone.

"Tracey and I split up last night," he told her.

Amelia gave a huge sigh. "I'm sorry," she said. "I hope it wasn't because of me."

"Only partly."

Amelia nodded. Further explanations seemed pointless.

"I want you back," he told her.

"I want you too."

Amelia took Kevin into the living room. The curtains were closed and it was pitch black. She turned on the Christmas tree lights. Warm colours filled the room – orange and red and green and gold. Soon they were on the sofa, embracing.

"I love you," she told Kevin. "I'll always love you. We won't go wrong this time. We won't let anyone get in our way."

Before she could finish her speech, Kevin began to tickle her, the way he used to when they were kids together. He wasn't going to let her get all passionate and dramatic on him. He'd had enough of that stuff yesterday. Amelia giggled and pushed him off her.

"We'd better get one thing clear," Kevin said, solemnly. "We're only going out with each other on a trial basis. And this time it's me who decides when the trial's over. Agreed?"

"Agreed," said Amelia.

Amelia would say whatever he wanted her to say. She knew he didn't mean it. Anyway, she was ready to prove her love. Amelia kissed Kevin on the chest, then told him, playfully, "No one'll be getting up for hours. We won't be disturbed."

Kevin kissed her again. Soon they were holding each other closer than either of them had been held before. *This must be what they call rapture*, Amelia thought, as they kissed hungrily, making up for lost time in the warm light cast by the Christmas tree. *This is what I was waiting to feel ready for.*

"If you don't have something with you," Amelia told Kevin, "I do."

Kevin shook his head.

"It's not time yet," he told her.

Amelia wasn't sure whether he was saying what she thought he was saying.

"What do you mean?"

Kevin kissed her neck. Then he spoke softly but firmly. "You may be ready for this, but I'm not sure if I am. And I want to be. I'm not like Rick, or Andy, and I'm going to prove it to you. I'm in this for the long run."

He paused, then added, "Let's wait a while."

Amelia kissed him softly on the forehead. She thought she understood. She knew that she loved

Kevin more than ever, and that she wouldn't stop wanting him. But he didn't know that. He had to be sure of her. She owed him that. The important thing was that, somehow, they were back together again.

"I love you," she told him once more, hoping he'd say it back to her.

"Nah, you don't," Kevin teased, gently. "You only want me for my body, you ... you cradle snatcher!"

They laughed, then pressed each other close again. Shards of warm, many-coloured light played on their embracing bodies. In the cool and tranquil dawn, neither one of them saw the shadow of another parting.

Coming soon from Point Romance . . .

New Year's Eve

by Caroline B. Cooney

The third book in Caroline B. Cooney's thrilling and romantic series about the lives and loves of five young girls . . .

"What do you want to talk about?"

"Families," Matt said promptly. "Next year. Life. Future."

"Oh, Matt, no! Not tonight! Let's just have a Happy New Year. Nothing heavy." She struggled to get comfortable in his lap. "Matt, you're quivering all over! What's the matter?"

"I have a fever."

"Oh, no, why didn't you say so?" Emily tried to sit up.

"I'm all heated up over you," he said, laughing.

She let go of all her muscles until she was a velvet puddle on top of him. "Matthew O'Connor, get to the point. First you're lost. Now you have a fever. Do you think your first love is getting out of hand?"

"Who says it's first love?" he teased. "I'll have you know I am a very experienced man."

"You'd better be precisely as experienced as I am, no more and no less. If you've been feverish elsewhere, you're in trouble, Matthew O'Connor."

"I'm in trouble when you call me by my whole name anyway. That's how I know you're mad at me."

"I'm not mad. I just want to dance through the evening. If we talk about where I'm going to live and how my family has fallen apart, I'll cry. Who needs that?"

"Which is why I want to talk about it," Matt said. He sat up so suddenly she practically rolled onto the floor.

"It's a good thing nobody can see us back here behind the piano." Emily muttered. "I have never looked so un-graceful in my life."

"You look perfect. I want to talk family."

"No, Matt! I can't bear talking about selfish, unkind, uncaring—"

"I mean us," Matt said

"Us?"

"Our family, Em, Yours and mine."

"Matt," she protested, "you and I aren't a family."

"We could be, though."

Emily was aware of every texture in the lounge. A voice speaking into a phone placed a rental car order; the piano played a slow rag; a glass was set down on the bar. The upholstery beneath her was nubbly and Matt smelled of his father's aftershave. Her heart was pounding so hard that the crimson ribbon at the top of her gown trembled.

Matt held her hand. Hers was like ice; his was hot as fever. There was something in his hand, and at first she thought it was a salted nut, that he was offering her something to eat.

It was a ring.

A lovely tiny diamond that sparkled in his palm like a thousand, thousand snow flakes.

"M&M," Matt whispered, "let's get married."

P●INT CRiME

If you like Point Horror, you'll love Point Crime!

A murder has been committed . . . Whodunnit?
Was it the teacher, the schoolgirl, or the best friend? An exciting new series of crime novels, with tortuous plots and lots of suspects, designed to keep the reader guessing till the very last page.

School for Death
Peter Beere
When the French teacher is found, drowned in the pond, Ali and her friends are plunged into a frightening night-mare. Murder has come to Summervale School, and *anyone* could be the next victim . . .

Shoot the Teacher
David Belbin
Adam Lane, new to Beechwood Grange, finds himself thrust into the middle of a murder investigation, when the headteacher is found shot dead. And the shootings have only just begun . . .

The Smoking Gun
Malcolm Rose
When David Rabin is found dead, in the school playing-field, his sister Ros is determined to find the murderer. But who would have killed him? And why?

Look out for:

Baa Baa Dead Sheep
Jill Bennett
Mr Lamb, resident caretaker of the *Tree Theatre*, has been murdered, and more than one person at the theatre had cause to hate him . . .

Avenging Angel
David Belbin
When Angelo Coppola is killed in a hit-and-run accident, his sister, Clare, sets out to find his killer . . .

Point Horror

Read if you dare. . . .

Are you hooked on horror? Are you thrilled by fear? Then these are the books for you. A powerful series of horror fiction designed to keep you quaking in your shoes.

Also in the Point Horror series:

Mother's Helper
by A. Bates

April Fools
The Lifeguard
Teacher's Pet
Trick or Treat
by Richie Tankersley Cusick

My Secret Admirer
by Carol Ellis

Funhouse
The Accident
The Invitation
The Window
The Fever
The Train
by Diane Hoh

Thirteen
by Christopher Pike, R.L. Stine and others

Beach Party
The Baby-sitter
The Baby-sitter II
The Boyfriend
The Snowman
The Girlfriend
Hit and Run
Beach House
The Hitchhiker
by R.L. Stine

The Cheerleader
The Return of the Vampire
The Perfume
by Caroline B. Cooney

The Waitress
by Sinclair Smith

The Cemetery
by D.E. Athkins

THE BABYSITTERS CLUB

Need a babysitter? Then call the Babysitters Club. Kristy Thomas and her friends are all experienced sitters. They can tackle any job from rampaging toddlers to a pandemonium of pets. To find out all about them, read on!

Look out for:

THE UNDERWORLD TRILOGY
Peter Beere

When life became impossible for the homeless of London many left the streets to live beneath the earth. They made their homes in the corridors and caves of the Underground. They gave their home a name. They called it UNDERWORLD.

UNDERWORLD
It was hard for Sarah to remember how long she'd been down there, but it sometimes seemed like forever. It was hard to remember a life on the outside. It was hard to remember the real world. Now it seemed that there was nothing but creeping on through the darkness, there was nothing but whispering and secrecy.

And in the darkness lay a man who was waiting to kill her . . .

UNDERWORLD II
"Tracey," she called quietly. No one answered. There was only the dark threatening void which forms Underworld. It's a place people can get lost in, people can disappear in. It's not a place for young girls whose big sisters have deserted them. Mandy didn't know what to do. She didn't know what had swept her sister and her friends from Underworld. All she knew was that Tracey had gone off and left her on her own.

UNDERWORLD III
Whose idea was it? Emma didn't know and now it didn't matter anyway. It was probably Adam who had said, "Let's go down and look round the Underground." It was something to tell their friends about, something new to try. To boast that they had been inside the secret Underworld, a place no one talked about, but everyone knew was there.

It had all seemed like a great adventure, until they found the gun . . .